PHLOGISTICS

OF A

SIMPLE MAN

OTHER WORKS BY TODD SHERMAN

Pitching Ice Cubes at the Sun: a Book of the Dead

Opals for Libras

Kong Hong

Paralytic States

Fluid Babies

Rise, Osiris!

PHLOGISTICS
OF A
SIMPLE MAN

TODD SHERMAN

Cover photo: Anna Mann

Book design: Melissa Hindle-Sherman

ISBN: 1514108003
ISBN-13: 978-1514108000

For the old timers who let me sit at their table.

YLEM

Steven Shaw left his house through the front door. He usually exits through the back because that's where he always parks. But last night there had been a storm. And whenever there was a storm, it meant that Steve had to pick up several small and large branches from the lawn. The lawn was greener, lusher than the day before. The lightning had flashed for a good two hours. Steve followed the random trail of twigs and branches around the side of his house, past the rhododendron bush that his ex-wife had planted many years ago. It sat wet with rain and vied for attention with its little pink buds. Steve continued to gather branches in his backyard. He made multiple trips to the burning barrel, throwing the severed limbs beside it into a makeshift pile. The grass was wet and he could feel the water seep through his sneakers, socks, into skin. The lawn needed cut. The rain made it grow so fast he couldn't keep up. He'd wait until it dried out some to mow it. The neighbor's lawn needed cut, too. The grass tickled the white metal doors of a rusted Camaro. It would go on tickling the car until it was covered in snow. Steve's neighbor never weed-whacked that far back. That was no man's land. Steve finished up piling the branches. He'd burn them later when everything dried out. He could already feel the stirring of the sun's warm rays.

He brushed his hands on jeans before climbing into his truck. He started the vehicle, caught his reflection in the rearview before backing out of the driveway. A cowlick stuck up from the back of his head. He licked his hand and tried to mat it down, but it wouldn't stay. It popped up twice before Steve gave up the struggle, screwing the cap from the passenger seat on his head full of rebellious hair. It would take a couple more weeks for the cowlick to grow out. The barber had cut his hair too short.

Onto the dirt road that ran parallel to his house, Steve slowly pulled himself toward his job waiting patiently through the dawn in the next town. The trunk bumped and dipped from the potholes created by past winters' wrath. Steve peered through his window at a neighborhood dog chained to a doghouse. It was perched atop a rusted-out burning barrel cut in half and filled with earth. The dog watched placidly as Steve drove by, licking his chops. Sometimes he did that. Sometimes he'd bark. Steve could never anticipate which demeanor he'd adopt. But the dog always watched him pass. Every morning on his way to work. Whether it was some form of misapplied loyalty or just plain stupidity, Steve couldn't tell.

He took a right at the end of the dirt road, ignored the DO NO ENTER sign and climbed up the wrong-way of a one-way street connecting a volunteer fire department's lot. It was early in the morning. No parked cars. None cruising down the lane. It saved Steve about two minutes to not have to loop all the way around to get to this point.

Left onto the main route and almost a straight shot to work. Sun glare breached the driver-side window making Steve squint just to see the road. He flipped the visor down and over, the eyes blinking a few times. Then a glide down the route at a comfortable forty mph, glancing side to side at the surroundings constantly receding into the past. These were some of the best moments in the day for Steve. Right before work on a leisurely drive at a leisurely pace calmly spying on the inhabitants wakening in the quiet town.

To the right, a Paki raked gravel at the end of his driveway. Steve took his foot off the accelerator. The driveway was perfectly even, rising at a slight incline, each stone in its proper place. A picnic could be had on that driveway if one wasn't too fussy about mussing up the gravel from spreading out the blanket. Steve sailed by and watched in the mirror's past the dark-haired, brown-skinned man working unperturbed with the rake. Steve imagined the man whistling. Steve smiled, easing back onto the gas.

The sun was shining and Steve felt pretty good.

THE EVERYDAY SINK-IN

Steve walked into the break room at his workplace and waved to the guys in the first row of the first table. Ted, Ozzie and Dave waved, nodded and waved back.

"What's going on, guys?" Steve said.

"Not much," Ozzie said.

"Hey," Ted said.

Dave just held up his coffee and gave a few rapid nods.

"Did you see the game last night?" Ted said.

"Yeah." Steve passed the table. "Lousy bums couldn't beat French Creek Valley Christian on their best

11

day."

The three guys chuckled and laughed and chuckled. Steve deposited change into the coffee machine: large size, light cream, heavy sugar.

"Del Rey looked good, though," someone from the back said.

Steve turned around. "Well, sure, Del Rey looked good, he always looks good. But what's the point of getting on base if the rest of the team don't bring the bats? Leave him stranded every fucking time."

"Guess you're right," the person said.

Steve bent down to pick up his coffee.

"I wouldn't make too light of French Creek Valley," Ozzie said. "Dora drops the kid off there. You should see him. He can smack the shit out of a Wiffle ball."

Ted chuckled, Dave grunted and Ted just chuckled again.

"I know, that's what I'm saying," Steve said. "They suck ass this year." He headed back toward the table with his coffee.

"Except for Del Rey," the person in the back said. "He looks good."

"That's already been established," Ted said.

Dave grunted again.

Steve sat down with his coffee and took a sip. Then Ted took a sip and Ozzie and Dave in their turns.

"This coffee tastes like shit," Ozzie said.

"It's not so bad." Steve with another sip.

"It's not so good either," Ted said.

Ozzie followed Ted with a sip.

Dave grunted and sipped.

Steve-Ted-Ozzie-Dave, Steve-Ted-Ozzie-Dave. None of them were conscious of the quadrilateral pattern they created. If any one of them had caught on, however, none would sip for a good three minutes. Then the coffee would start to get cold and the cycle would renew itself in exactly the same order. And they'd have forgotten all over again the quadrilateral with its sipping sequence. None taking a real mouthful.

The door swung open. In walked the man with the sandwich in his hand. He pointed a finger at the guys. They waved, nodded, sipped, grunted back.

"Hey, hey, what's up, guys?" he said.

"Not much, Donnie," Steve said.

"Nothing," Ozzie said.

Donnie strode by with the plastic-wrapped sub. "Boy, aren't you guys cheery today?" He opened the fridge and plopped his lunch on a wire-rack shelf.

"Yeah."

"So?"

Grunts and sipping.

Donnie slammed the fridge door. "What's shaking, Sammy?"

And the guy in the back just blushed. "Uh . . ." Sammy, the cafeteria stowaway, looked outside. "Nothing."

"Well, all right." Donnie spun around and practically strutted toward the pop machine.

"What, did you get laid last night?" Ted said.

Steve turned and grinned with a bellyful of warm coffee.

"Shutting up for something," Ozzie said. "So, Donnie, get yourself some pussy last night?"

Donnie picked up the can of Mountain Dew and cracked it. He scanned the room. There weren't any females present. "Well, you know how it is, guys."

"You fucking dog." Ted shaking his head.

Donnie dragged a sip, slipped toward the table and the guys with their lukewarm paper-cupped coffees. He dropped into a chair across from Steve. A night full of memories pasted his lips into a blood-gorged smile.

"Well, what about you guys?" Donnie looked around the table. "Tell me you didn't just sit around watching the game all night?"

Steve and Ted and Ozzie and Dave shot glances at each other. Then they sipped their drinks in a hurried cycle.

"Oh, come on now," Donnie said. "You watched the game?"

"Well, they were playing the Reds," Ozzie said. "It's a division game, man, we had to watch."

"But it was a snoozer. I mean even early on." Donnie looked from guy to guy. "Are you telling me you couldn't at least've got a quick zap in?"

Ted flicked the plastic tab on the cover to his coffee with an unclipped thumbnail. Ozzie considered a freckle between his thumb and forefinger. Dave almost growled; the sound of his usual grunt, only stretched out.

Steve cleared his throat. "Not all of us have the time to get a quick zap in. Some of us have other priorities." Steve nodded to Ted and Ozzie and Dave. "Some of us have wives."

"And mine actually gets in the way of having sex," Ted said.

"Dora uses the baby as an excuse." Ozzie lost in the little red dot on his hand. "Either we'll wake it or it's crying and needs fed or the diaper's full of shit."

Dave grunted and scratched the stubble on his chin.

"Jesus, you guys are pathetic." Donnie shook his head then downed his soda.

"Well, I'll tell you what," Steve said. "Why don't you give us all of the details so that we can live vicariously through you, Superstud."

Donnie's face crinkled, swallowing hard so Mountain Dew wouldn't spray all over the guys and the table. His eyes watered but he gained control. "You horny old bastard, I bet you'd like to know."

"Was she a blonde?" Ozzie asked.

"Why don't you go change a diaper, Nanny Oz?"

Steve and Ted busted out laughing. Ozzie held

back his coffee cup, almost passing the boundary between self-redemption and lunch-room etiquette. He reddened, grinned and muttered a short list of curses into his cup as he set it on the table. Even Dave had chuckled a few times between the grunts.

"She was a redhead. And she had big old titties out to here." Donnie was beaming with his hands full of imaginary tit. "D-cup, I'd say. And she fucked like a porn queen."

"Yeah, yeah," Steve said. "They all fuck like porn queens."

"No, they all don't," Donnie said. He pointed at his chest. "Just the ones I'm with."

"Uh huh." Steve sipped his coffee.

"And they all leave satisfied."

"Uh huh."

"And sore."

"And dwarfed by your ego."

"At least I'm getting some."

"You ain't getting dick."

"That's right," Donnie said. "I ain't getting dick." He set his empty can on the table with a significant ting. "But enough about me. How about you, Steve? When was the last time you tagged it? Was it before or after Bradshaw was quarterback?"

The guys laughed.

Steve snorted. "I've had more pussy than you'll ever get to smell."

The guys laughed even louder.

Donnie shook his head, smiling. "All right, old timer, all right, you win." He hook shot his empty Mountain Dew can into the trash bin. "What should we talk about then? The game?"

A few moments of silence. Most of the guys looked unsure as to whether they should be uneasy or angry. So Donnie drummed a fast rhythm with fingers on the worn cafeteria table. Steve picked up a Sears flyer from yesterday's paper.

"Damn shame that game was," Ted said. Broke the silence too early. He traced the imitation grain pattern of the table. "Damn shame."

"Only embarrassed themselves," Ozzie said.

Donnie kept drumming.

Dave grunted.

Steve half-heartedly scanned the flyer for bargains on things he wasn't ever going to buy.

"Del Rey looked good." Sammy said, stashed in the back with the old magazines, plastic plates from past birthday parties and a faint trickle of salt that curiously never seemed to fall from the table.

Donnie stopped drumming. He whipped around. "Did you score last night, Sammy?"

"What?" Sammy turned red.

"Ever tickle the cleft chin?" Donnie grinning demon-wise from over the edge of the plastic chair. "A man your age can't be a virgin."

The guys laughing. Donnie smiled at them and turned back to Sammy, but Sammy had his mouth clamped shut.

"You're not a virgin, are you?" Donnie asked.

Sammy watched a bird flying that wasn't really there. His face stop sign red.

Ozzie snickered. "Come on, Sammy, you can tell them." He looked at the guys, nodded toward Sammy. "He had my grandmother last night."

The guys laughed.

"Kept me up all night," Ozzie said. "All those sloppy sucking sounds."

"Jesus Christ, you're sick," Steve said between laughs.

"I thought your grandmother was dead," Ted said.

"She is, but last night she was resurrected and crucified all over again."

The guys laughed with disgusted faces, all wishing they could stop themselves from laughing at such a horrible thought. But necrophilia and grandma jokes are funny.

And all the time their coffees grew cold. Had forgotten all about them. Had forgotten to sip in turns. Their attentions centered on a fresh hot subject that sat red and staring at nothing not more than fifteen feet away. A fresh hot subject. Fresh only in the daily sense. Month upon month, year in and year out, Sammy blushed from the guys' blunt verbal pokers. More monkey-in-a-cage than co-worker.

"Del Rey looked good," was all Sammy could say. And that's why he was a monkey.

The guys laughed again, as usual.

Ozzie muttering, "Fucking virgin."

And Ted even lower, "Fucking loser."

Then the cafeteria door flew open, two women talking as they walked into the room, talking loud, near-yelling, maybe compensating for the machines screaming and banging out past the door. And so they china-bulled onto the scene, as they did every morning. The guys had quickly drowned laughter into recently remembered coffees. Donnie picked up the drum pattern about where he'd left it. Nothing left for him to drink.

"How's it going, guys?" The first loud woman.

"Hey, Carla," Steve said.

And then in order:

"Hey, Carla." Ted

"Hey, Carla." Ozzie.

Grunt, grunt. Dave.

"Hey, Carla." Donnie.

Stifled laughter, dancing smiles, table-gazing from the guys. Carla followed their bursts and near eruptions to Sammy. And then back to the guys.

"You guys picking on poor Sammy?" she said.

The guys feigned ignorance. Suppressed

17

explosions and shrugs.

Ted coughed. "What do you mean?"

"You know exactly what I mean." Carla turned to the woman behind her.
She just rolled her eyes.

"Just sitting here drinking our coffee," Ozzie said.

"Uh huh."

"Hey, Vickie," Steve said.

"Hey," she said back.

Carla and Vickie hung at the door a moment, looking at the guys, shaking heads and scrunching faces. They headed toward the refrigerator.

"You guys catch the game last night?" Carla asked.

"Yeah," Steve said.

And then:

"Yeah."

"Yeah."

Grunt.

"Not me." Donnie almost beaming. He kept drumming.

Carla dropped her lunch onto the shelves. Vickie patiently waited her turn. Sammy sat to the side of them. He wasn't looking out the window. He seemed to have forgotten about the bird that wasn't really there.

"Boy, they sure got the crap beat out of them," Carla said, trading places with Vickie.

"Yeah."

"Yeah."

"Yeah."

Grunt.

Drumming.

"Del Rey looked good, though," Sammy said.

The guys exploded and the table shook with their laughter. Steve holding his gut, Ted crying, Ozzie banging the table with his free hand. And somehow Dave had unwittingly crushed his coffee cup. Brown liquid seeped through his fingers and fanned out on the table. Donnie pointed at Dave and laughed and Dave laughed and Steve held his gut and laughed while Ozzie bounced the table in place with a pounding fist and Ted crying, crying, crying with his head on the table.

"Now what the hell's gotten into you guys?" Vickie closed the fridge and looked to Carla.

"I think they've been picking on Sammy again." Carla's arms folded. "They been picking on you, Sammy?"

Sammy found another imaginary bird.

Carla's hard eyes on the table. "You guys are cruel, you know that? Why don't you just leave him alone?"

"Pathetic," Vickie said.

The guys kept laughing. Dave wiping the table off before the liquid could run into Ted's hat. Laughing grunts bursting from him the whole time. Muffled sounds from Ted's buried face. Steve's jiggling belly slowly grinding itself to a halt.

"Why don't you grow up?" Carla passed them by and exited the cafeteria.

Ozzie would start up every now and then before settling back into quietude, rubbing the side of his red hand. And Donnie up at the vending machine again, buying another Mountain Dew to bring out to the floor. Pop in hand, sputtering, rolling toward the door.

"You guys are fucking imbeciles." Vickie at the guys' table with a cup of tea.

Donnie turned back before leaving. "Aw, come on, Vickie, give it a rest, will you?"

She spun around. "Shut the hell up, you little cock."

"It's bigger than you are." Donnie smiling.

"Hey."

"Better watch it."

"Jesus, man."

The death-stare broken, Vickie blew past Donnie,

out the door into the workplace's machine cattle call. The guys laughed and wagged fingers at Donnie.

"You guys working today?" Donnie asked.

Steve glanced at the clock. "Yeah, I suppose it's that time." He got up.

"Who lit the fire under your guys' ass?" Ozzie turned to Dave. "It's not even seven yet."

Dave shrugged and grunted.

Steve was on the floor in his department standing in front of his press. The previous press operator unloaded parts. Steve got his stuff together: gloves, mask, extra press log sheets. He scanned the paperwork, the tickets. He filled out a time sheet and threw his clipboard on a filing cabinet. Finally, he leaned against a wall in front of the monitor in front of the press and waited for the operator to finish. Steve would stay leaning like this for a good part of the day.

"Hey, how's it going, Steve?" The operator walked up to the console with the flashy monitor.

"Good, how about you?"

"Good."

Time passing and the operator nodding his head.

"How's the press running?" Steve said.

"Good, good, no problems."

Steve pointed at a sheet of paper lying on the console's keyboard. "I thought we were done with substrate."

"Yeah, well, that's the end of it there." The operator indicated the rack full of parts to be loaded. "It's a rush order. Really hot."

Steve shrugged. "All right."

More time passing and Steve watching the little icons and objects on the screen. The operator beside him found something interesting there, too. Then he turned to Steve.

"Did you see the game last night?" he asked.

"I'd rather not talk about it."

"Know what you mean, what a clobbering."

And still time passed. That same damn interesting thing on the screen again; bright red and stagnant for the next 19.3 minutes.

"Haji was out raking today," Steve said.

"Again?"

"Uh huh."

"How many days in a row does that make?"

"I don't know," Steve said. He put his hands in his work jacket. "Probably two months now. Ever since he moved in."

"Man, that's strange."

"Yeah."

The operator looked at the clock on the screen. "Hey, it's past my shift. I'm getting the hell out of here."

"All right."

"See you tomorrow."

"Yeah, see you."

The door to another room closed as the operator left. A sign on the door: WARNING: WEAR PERSONAL PROTECTIVE EQUIPMENT. Steve adjusted his safety glasses and glanced over at the thermometer on the wall he leaned against. Seventy-two degrees Fahrenheit. He looked back at the screen with his hands in the pockets of his work jacket. The jacket powder blue and flame resistant. Steve stayed far enough from the press's heat anyway. He wouldn't get burned. In fact, the computer showed Steve that he wouldn't have to even move for the next fifteen minutes.

When Steve finally did move, it was in this order:

put on gloves

pull out die

lay out parts on cooling table next to previous cycle's parts

push in die

make up new die for next transfer

punch out previous cycle's parts

bring parts into adjacent room

take off gloves

lean against wall

Occasionally, a fellow employee would come up and bullshit with Steve for ten minutes before the next transfer when Steve would have to move. This happened every day for the last twenty-eight years. And Steve didn't mind it. The pay was good. The benefits were good. He got along with most everybody. Things were smooth and safe and comfortable for all the high voltage signs and pinch point labels. And he was leaning. And not thinking of the game last night. He was thinking about fishing for bass.

BITCHES AND BLACK MEN

Steve and Ted and Ozzie and Dave and Donnie were in the cafeteria for lunch. Other people were in the room, but at different tables. Sammy wasn't there. He always took lunch a half hour after everyone else. He preferred to eat alone. For obvious reasons.

Steve spooned in chili that he'd purchased from the vending machine. Ted took his chances on an AVI special: The Big Texan's two big beef patties, buns, onions and a generous pickle. Ozzie dealt with his usual ham and cheese sandwiches; sparse squares pressed flat and unornamented by lettuce, tomato or dressing. Dave grunted over a bowl of corn chowder. They all had Cokes. Except for Donnie. He drank a Mountain Dew with his bag of chips. But that was OK. He was still one of the guys. He didn't have to drink Coke.

"Those look like they came from the pre-press," Steve said, pointing his spoon at Ozzie's pathetic sandwiches.

"Goddamn wife, don't know why she does it," Ozzie said. "I tell her not to squish them like that—not to put the apple on top of everything, but she doesn't listen."

"They're thin as crackers, for Christ's sake."

"I know."

"Could use them as Frisbees."

"I know already." Ozzie took a bite. Most of his sandwich disappeared.

"Women have to be put in their place," Donnie said. He popped in a fresh tortilla and crunched.

"And what the hell would you know about it?" Ozzie said. "You've never kept a woman long enough to know what they want."

"Oh, I know." Donnie smiling and crunching. "That's why I don't have anything steady right now. None of them were the right kind. Once the mystery wears off, they only want you around so they can control you. Sooner or later they all turn out to be bitches."

"They're all bitches," Steve said. He grimaced. The chili wasn't sitting well.

"You're such a romantic, Donnie." A woman a few tables away. She went back to her salad.

Donnie shrugged. "Hey." He pointed his can at Ozzie. "You've got to put your foot down, got to tell her to make your sandwiches the way you like them. No more squishing, no more apples on top. I mean, you're the man of the house, aren't you? You're the one bringing home the check every week."

"She works, too," Ozzie said.

"She does?"

"Why do you think we drop the kid off downtown in the mornings?"

"Oh." Donnie paused with a chip in his hand. "But that doesn't matter, you're still the man. You've got to lay down the law, set the standard, not her." He swallowed the chip. "If you don't stand up for yourself in small situations like these, she'll walk all over you every time, guaranteed."

"It's not that easy," Ozzie said. He picked up his second sadly squished sandwich.

Donnie's hands up. "Why not? Sounds to me like you make it harder for yourself than it has to be."

"He's right, Donnie." Steve stirring the remains of his chili. "Marriage is about compromise and sacrifice. It's easy for you to say what you say and believe it because you're too young to know the difference. But you'll know someday, and on that day you'll keep your thoughts to yourself."

"Listen to you." The same woman from the back. "How'd you get wise? Tell me, why is it then that you're divorced if you know so much about marriage?"

The room grew silent.

"But you are right about one thing," Steve finally said. "They're all bitches." Steve didn't move and didn't take his eyes away from Donnie.

Ozzie leaned over to Donnie and said real low, "They'll fucking castrate you, swear to God." Ozzie nibbled at his sandwich.

Ted hadn't eaten anything for a while. The conversation fed his appetite. He seemed perplexed and lifted his face from his food to Ozzie.

"Why don't you just pack your own lunch?" he said.

The lady from the table busted out laughing. The guys grew quiet. Everyone at the table fidgeted with their meals. Everyone except for Ozzie. He stuffed the last three-quarters of squished sandwich into his mouth. It didn't matter. Ozzie still turned red. He grabbed his Coke and could hardly wait for the food to be broken down enough to swallow. It took a while. He nearly choked.

Steve finished his chili. He cleared his throat. Maybe he meant to say something. Maybe he thought better of it and decided to keep his trap shut. And then it could've just been acid in his gut. He polished off his Coke and yet there was still something trying to get out. An idea, maybe, fighting upstream against the descending corn syrup flow. The carbonation made his eyes water. It was the only time he ever appeared to be crying. In this room. And the painful twist to his face seemed a reaction to the fighting salmon. But it was just the bubbles. Or the chili.

Donnie blew air threw pursed lips.

Dave was nonexistent. Not even grunting.

"Hey, did you guys happen to see the new engineer?" She'd twisted the knife enough. "He's touring some of the shops. Maybe he'll come around your way."

"A new engineer?" Steve rubbed at the water in one of his eyes. "Did someone quit?"

"No," the woman said. "Someone got canned."

"Who?"

"Tordella."

Ted looked up. "So, he finally got caught, huh?"

"Yep."

And that's where the matter was left. Tordella was never spoken of again. Wouldn't be long before everybody forgot he'd ever existed. At least by the people in the lunch room. And the lunch room was where memories died last in the work shop. This one a quick and graceless fade.

"And you guys will love him." The woman's grin that unkind dagger.

"Oh, yeah?" Steve said. "And why's that?"

"He's black."

Ozzie had already swallowed hard and was still recovering from that. His face baby-ass pink all over. He breathed and shook his head. "They hired a black guy?"

"There goes the shop," Ted said.

"I don't have anything against a black engineer working here," Steve said.

The woman in the back sniggered. "Yeah, right."

"So long as he's not lazy like the others they'd hired before." Steve brushed a tear from his other eye and then let out a monstrous belch.

The woman shook her head. "You always have to be such a pig?"

"Uh huh," Steve said.

Ozzie turned to Steve. "They had black guys working here once?"

Steve nodded.

"Goddamn coons," Ted said. "They're everywhere."

"I don't know." Donnie straightened himself in his chair. "Sounds like it could be good. We could use some diversity around here—a little bit of color." Donnie grinned—the guy who drank Mountain Dew. "I'm kind of sick of looking at you pale-faced bastards, anyway."

"Shut the fuck up, Donnie," Ozzie said. "You're just as white as the rest of us."

Steve out of the building and heading for his truck. A little metal cap sat upside down in his path. He kicked it and kicked it again, following his quarry in a meandering course through the parking lot. No one else was around, so he didn't have to worry about getting out of anyone's way. Twenty minutes after his shift. He liked to take his time cleaning up and he liked not to have to fight with traffic getting on the main route to his house. He kicked the bottle cap and kicked it again and so had in time reached his vehicle. An idea popped into his head. A slight frown to the face. Steve bent down to pick up the little metal object. It wasn't a beer cap. Cream soda. Understanding seemed to flood Steve's eyes and so he flicked the cap beyond his truck bed into the grass-lined ditch behind the asphalt. He knew that he couldn't have ever been that careless.

Steve climbed into his truck. He pulled out a bottle of beer from the cooler on the floor. There wasn't any ice in the cooler, so the bottle wasn't cold. But it had been out of the sun and Steve always left the windows down on nice days. It was a nice day. Steve scanned the parking lot and popped the top to his bottle. He took a long drink before starting the engine. The beer sat between his legs as he surveyed the surroundings. He'd heard that a beer a day was good for you. Helped clean out the blood. Everyday after work Steve cleaned out the day's toxins from his blood. He let his foot off the brake and started to roll down the slight decline.

And then a tiny jolt. He'd reapplied the brakes. In the distance was a dark figure striding along the walkway separating Steve's plant from another directly opposite. A black-skinned man. He wore a gray polo shirt, black pants and dress shoes. The new engineer. Tall and thin and walking with a certain hidden power under that gray polo and black skin.

Steve hit the bottle again. The brown glass cylinder attached to his face blurred as he looked beyond it to the grounds of his workplace. He spotted the man walking, paying him no special attention until the dark head suddenly spun around. Steve dropped the bottle to his lap and coughed forcefully. Startled, eyes watering and the beer down the wrong pipe. The black engineer was looking at Steve. Or at least in his direction. He turned his head back and continued walking. Couldn't have known from this distance that Steve was drinking a beer. So he let off the brake, added a little gas and coasted down the parking lot. He took the corner and watched obliquely the black man reach the shop's door. Was he looking at him drive past? Steve didn't think so. He took a right and hooked onto the road leading to route 198 which in turn brought him to his house and his bathroom on the second level where he'd piss out the beer he'd finished on the journey home.

Steve would've been rummaging through his refrigerator if there'd been anything at all to rummage. Instead, he scanned the starved shelves and shuffled the half-gallon of out-dated milk back and forth a couple times. He closed the door and made his way to the dining room table. The mail lay where he'd placed it. He had no desire to open any of it. The Capital One envelope remained sealed and the current Watchtower pamphlet left by some well-meaning Jehovite went unread. The insurance bill he had to open. So he opened it. And of course the bill was due five days from now. He'd tried and tried to straighten them out, but they just couldn't be straightened. Calls and complaints and personal visits proved ineffective so he simply gave in to the predestined paperwork glitch. When in doubt, give in. He always paid it the day he'd received it so it didn't matter anyway. And he always pitched the mail that he left sealed and unread.

Steve was hungry. His gurgling belly only confirmed what his aching body already knew. He needed food and he needed it quick. So Steve grabbed his wallet and keys, snatched the insurance bill that didn't need to be paid for five days and hauled his ass downtown to fill his ever-gurgling gut.

He kept the windows down in his truck. It was a nice day. He'd already had his beer. The toxins had been flushed. He could begin the cycle anew of filling his veins with crap. It was his other favorite time of the day. Where tomorrow's concerns were tomorrow's concerns and the salt and cheese and carcinogenic meat could pile up in unwatched deposits.

He passed through varying sounds strung across the street in the invisible thread of spiders. An unseen vehicle honked from somewhere far away, laughter of children swayed in the wind, the rush of cars passed by, breaking the invisible thread, a random stereo blasted much too loudly with too much bass, a shout from one side of the street to the other. Steve's eyes roamed freely over all of the area. His arm braced within the window frame of the door while free fingers tapped against the roof. The sounds all around him snapped like string and he was conscious of their breaking and fading away. Fingers tapping and he could hear and see the town shift by as he sped his way down the main route.

The bowling alley came into view on the right and fell away. Kentucky Fried Chicken and then Pizza Hut popped up on the left and drowned in a wave of concrete. Steve's truck churned forward, over the hill, atop the bridge that circled past the Sewage Treatment plant and a

Taco Bell. Fortunately, it wasn't a hot day. The town's shit and piss were tolerable today. Steve watched other fast-food restaurants rise from the ground with homes, municipal buildings, auto parts stores, banks, beauty salons and other businesses wedged in between them. Around the curve Steve saw the streetlight turn yellow and knew he could make it through the intersection if the guy in front of him would speed up a little. But the guy stepped on the brakes instead, stopping ten feet from the white line.

"Oh, come on," Steve said. "We could've made it."

Steve tapped his roof impatiently. He inched toward the car in front of him. A group of high school girls in a red sports car slowed past Steve, stopping at the light in the adjacent lane. A car ahead of him and more and he could still hear their music. Some light, airy pop song with a weak female wisp accompanied by the teenagers' untrained voices. They were all soft skin and soft hair and soft lips. Enough head-shaking attitude to fool a thirteen year-old boy into believing they were in complete control of the world of men. War and peace and most definitely sex. So they shook their heads and smiled and sang until they maybe even fooled a forty-eight year-old man in a pick-up truck into believing they controlled the entire sexual sphere. Maybe sex. But no amount of shaking and singing and pouting and waving could convince anyone that they held any sway over war and peace. Certainly not those. War and peace were the by-products of the adult world and quite simply could not cram themselves into a car loaded with four gyrating high school girls.

The car behind them beeped and that's when Steve realized that he'd been staring at them the whole time, failing to notice himself that the light had turned green. He took off and glanced into the rearview and was glad to find that no one was there. The girls tailgated by the scowling driver behind them. Steve slowed down, allowing the car to switch into his lane and blast off toward the next stoplight. Steve wheeled his car over and stalked from behind. The girls had already forgotten about the rude little beep and sang and shook with even more coquettish vigor.

And then the next stoplight. They had already caught up to the impatient driver. He glowered at the girls, oblivious, lost irretrievably in the bang and bop of an obvious pop song. And they would continue their innocence, their clueless, happy existence even through the next green light. But for now they sang and slipped pink tips of tongues in and out over soft pink lips while Steve sat watching with a simmering lust. But only simmering. It was, quite frankly, too nice of a day to get too worked up about anything. The pop song floated from the car with the girls' feather voices, riding the gentle waves to the brutish blossom of Steve's ear. Unconscious that his fingers beat in time with the teen-scented music. Pheromones on the wind. He watched their hair fling and fall and even allowed them to ignore the stoplight. A car honked behind him and the girls awakened into reality, laughing and pushing onward. The impatient driver, of course, had long since smashed the accelerator with pent up testosterone; the by-product of being ignored by sixteen year-old vixens-to-be.

Steve followed them through the next light and the next light after that, took their turns, mimicked their curves, easily gelling with the soft plastic ass of their car. He dipped when they dipped, smiled when they smiled, breathed in the mild spring air as they shed estrogen in clouds of pollen. Eventually, they came to a stop sign. A busy street crosscut the road. The girls in the tight little sports car and Steve in a rumbling tank. But for now idling. Both of them. Traffic passed before them, carried away in the stream to some hidden nook of suburbia. They continued to sit at the sign for quite some time. Enough time for one of the girls to notice they were being watched by the guy in the pick-up behind them and that maybe they'd been followed and watched all along, for God knows how many streets. A blonde with sparkles in her eyes, looking back at Steve with a sophomoric cringe. Dirty old man on the pink tip of her tongue, mouthing something over and over. The other girl in back leered in disgust. Steve hardly even noticed them. Or so he played it. But if the girls had seen his fingers they'd have noticed them tapping madly on his truck's roof.

"OK, game's over."

He winked at the girls and flicked on his turn signal. A girl put her hands to her lips and stared in disbelief at her friend beside her. Then a gap in the traffic and the sports car pulled away, one sweetly flushed female scowling DIRTY OLD MAN, DIRTY OLD MAN at Steve. He in his turn veered onto the busy street and carried a smile evoked by the mild day and the memories of soft pink lips mouthing airy pop songs in his head.

Other things caught his attention, moving along the sidewalks. A fat woman carried groceries in sagging plastic bags, her bare thighs indistinguishable from the knees, rubbing forever together until they could sigh one last time on a sagging plastic-covered couch. A pole of a lady jogged in soccer shorts over spandex and a tank top holding breasts loosely against a frail chest. Steve eyed her in the rearview. A scarecrow in flight. And little kids trailed by mothers outside a chain-linked fence bordering the school grounds. A crossing guard blew her whistle and held out a hand to pedestrians-in-training. A balled-up man toiled down the street in stuttering steps and swings; muscles tensed in a body-long cramp. Cars passed by and he watched them. As he watched all life pass before his head jerked violently aside. And then life was the sidewalk with its cracks and litter and feet that shuffled away from him. Steve watched and pitied and felt his own stomach bunch up. The light ahead was green and soon Steve forgot about the man struggling with the cruel, broken march of the sidewalk. It was a mild day after all.

At one intersection, Steve happened to glance over at a man under the propped hood of an eighties beast of a car. The faded blue face of an auto shop shadowed the man plying his hands inside the monster's rough metal gullet. His legs dangled over the grill and thick-lipped bumper. He pulled himself from the mouth and retrieved a bottle of motor oil resting on the ground. The cap cracked and the bottle up to his nose. Breathing deeply, almost sighing. A brown arc marked the tip of his nose. He opened his eyes and saw Steve watching him. An angry face replaced the expression of motor-oiled bliss before he ducked under the hood with the bottle. His feet dangling, swallowed once again by the machine. Steve never bothered to look away until the light had changed.

Down the road a few blocks on the right stood Pizza Heaven. Chipped painted brick and a sign barely legible. Steve knew it from memory. Could've made his way blindfolded. He pulled into the parking lot and stopped at a leaning post, leaving the engine running. Into the joint, smiling, holding the door open for a guy with his pizza delivery bag.

"Thanks."

"No problem."

Behind the counter stood a middle-aged guy with an uncreased baseball cap. His face slack and oily. Too many hours spent in the pizza industry. He waited until Steve picked up a menu before betraying any hints of animation. A crumpled napkin scooped up from the counter and swiped across his shiny brow. He dropped the napkin back onto the counter and resumed his lifeless pose. But the sweat would've given him away. He didn't have to move or breath. Just melt and wait for the salty sting in the eyes. Or for a customer to say something.

So Steve said, "Boy, it's a nice day out."

"Yeah."

"This weather could last all through summer and I'd love it."

The man didn't reply. He sniffed. Maybe he could smell the salt gathering, ready to burst and flow again.

Steve's gaze fell to the counter as he scanned the menu. Pepperoni sounded good. But then again, pepperoni always sounded good. Beside the normal choices, a new list of exotic pizzas: Fajita Chicken Supreme pizza; the Jamaican Junk with jerk sauce and wasabi; the Californian with avocado, cucumber and TVP; the Safari Big Game pizza with elephant meat and ground rhino horn; the Hawaiian Baby Choker with fist-sized chunks of ham, pineapple rind and dismembered G.I. Joes. Steve wrinkled his nose.

"What's with the last two specials?" he asked.

"They're jokes, for the college crowd."

"Oh."

No need for outlandish fare. Steve preferred pepperoni. Straightforward, simple, tasty.

"I'll take a . . . fourteen inch pepperoni pizza." Steve pointed at the item on the menu.

The clerk didn't even look. Or blink. "You want regular crust?"

"Yeah."

"Is that it?"

"Yeah."

Scribbles on paper. "OK, fifteen minutes." He tore the order and placed it on a counter behind him.

"I'll be back," Steve said.

Stone-faced. Only scooping the napkin to wipe the grease from his forehead.

Steve exited the pizza shop, turning the corner and hopping into his truck. A turn of the key, a check of the clock, a folded piece of paper nipped from the visor. The insurance bill. He tossed it to the passenger seat and backed out of the lot onto the main street, blowing by the pizza joint and through the intersection, past a group of teenagers overladen with bulging backpacks and baggy clothing, faster and faster, beyond the cries, the little laughs, the muted shouts for human attention. And time slid along with him, the seconds growing fat with thoughts of pepperoni.

His truck squeezed through cars, filling the gap of a driveway before slipping its roaring body between straight white lines. Rumbles to a sigh. He burst from the steel belly, undigested, and walked along the sidewalk leading to the insurance office. Undigested but thirsty. He eyed the Country Fair across the street. Too many cars being pumped full of gas. And kids on bikes and skateboards and caffeinated drinks. A bony woman with a cigarette in her mouth yelled at her bony children to watch out for the cars, the other kids, the caffeine on wheels. Too many, too much. Steve wasn't that thirsty. He remembered that the pizza joint had two-liters of Coke. And so he turned away. A shot through the insurance building's glass door revealed nothing but a counter, a large plant next to it and a dark wall, maybe paneled, and maybe also with plaques and picture frames. Couldn't really tell from the outside. But the inside world seemed impossibly quiet, impossibly inert. He climbed the stairs, yanked open the door with the jangling bell and pierced the office's reek of cigarettes and freshly laid carpet. A gaze back through the door and the outside world glided by in its usual way; noisy and dangerous and overridden by angry rubber tread.

When Steve emerged, he had rid himself of a piece of paper. One less claw of the outside world stuck in his undigested flesh. Pepperoni slices spun in his head and Steve's tongue flicked between lips. A cold river of Coke slapped against the walls of his skull. He shivered and leapt back into his truck. Sliding wheeled beasts outside his window and soon Steve's truck was roaring, too. He backed up, glancing out his back window, and caught a flash of black skin, black pants, a gray shirt. The new engineer at Steve's shop. Steve knew it had to be, wiping his windshield clean with a squeegee. A handle stuck out from the fuel filler to a shiny new BMW. The black man rounded the front of the car to clean the passenger window. He hadn't seen Steve and that was good because Steve had been staring out the back of his truck for some time. The man's face wrinkled in concentration as he scrubbed at a spot several times. He went and dipped the squeegee into a container of cleanser. Steve watched the bright blue BMW, shiny and sharp and misplaced in an oasis stuffed with rusted and bulky American cars. Light glinted from the molding around the door and the black man returned to swipe the back window.

"How much does insurance on that run?" Steve said.

He turned around and pulled through the lot to the other side. Pizza was on his brain. Pepperoni sounded good. A cold wash of cola. Steve's mind slid into a coma of cheese-covered wheels, mozzarella strands to breaking point, the sweet meaty smells of corn syrup and burnt protein.

The Pirates were on TV and Steve sat facing it, on his couch, with the pizza box open and the pizza steam rising from the center of his coffee table. A half-eaten piece still loaded with pepperoni in his hand, perched in front of a smashing set of teeth. Cheese hung down from the sides. A long strand had oozed over a finger, drooping slowly toward the carpet of his living room floor. It burned his skin. But the pizza tasted so good. He swallowed and took another big bite; the fat teardrop of cheese lost in the crush of molars.

Del Rey on deck. Warbeck at bat and looking more and more inept with each swing and miss. Warbeck was in a slump. Warbeck was a bum. Steve chewed harder, willing his energy through the glass screen and into the overplump pipes of the batter. Warbeck connected with the ball and sent it over the fence, far left of the foul pole.

Steve waving his pizza. "Come on, you bum."

Warbeck kicked at the dirt, stretched his arms into the air while holding the bat, took three mighty swings and stepped back into the box. He spit and shot the pitcher a stare that meant he was going to split the fucker's skull open with a searing line drive. The pitcher appeared unworried. Warbeck was in a slump after all.

"Haven't done anything all season. Now come on, let's see some hitting." A couple huge chomps, right down to the knobby crust.

A mighty pitch, a mighty swing, a mighty whiff. The wind from the bat blew the pitcher's face into a smile. The batter thumped the turf and carried away the ineffective bludgeon over a slumped shoulder.

"What a bum."

Warbeck was a bum. But Del Rey was up to bat. Steve dropped the crust in the box and fished for another slice. He couldn't take his eyes from the screen. His mouth hung open in a stifled scream of expectation. Del Rey cracked his neck, tightened the grip on his colossal bat.

At that moment—that silent, supreme, sacred moment—the phone rang. A profaning, hateful sound. Steve tore himself from the TV. He got the phone after the third ring. The machine had picked up and was giving Steve's apology for not being there.

"Hello? Hello?"

Steve had to fumble with the buttons. The machine shut up and Steve was left in silence.

Cheers from the TV and Steve brought the phone into the living room with him.

"Hello . . . HELLO."

Del Rey jogging toward second base, fist in the air.

"Goddamn it."

A shot of the crowd in the bleachers with hats bobbing, banners twirling, foam fingers reaching for the sky.

"Hello . . . yeah, speaking."

Del Rey rounding second and smiling his way toward third.

"Yeah . . . look, I'm not interested. No."

Horns blaring, the commentator's grinning faces. All babbling about the homerun and how this was an opportunity for the team to capitalize on the momentum. Del Rey was the hottest hitter that season. No one remembered what a bum Warbeck was.

"I don't care. Put me on your DO-NOT-CALL list."

Steve hung up the phone with the guy on the other end mumbling how sorry he was about something-or-other that didn't matter. Del Rey hit a homerun. And Steve had missed it.

"Goddamn it!"

Steve almost threw the phone across the room, but he knew the clatter-smash of a broken plastic shell wouldn't satisfy. A few breaths and he went over to the base unit to gently click the phone back home. Then to the set to watch Del Rey slap hands in the dugout.

Simnel stepped up to bat. And he was a bum, too. At least this season. Steve plopped onto the couch, allowing the homerun to sink in and eventually ease out the crinkles in his face. He picked up a slice of pizza and didn't get burned by the cheese. It had cooled down enough. The heat had dissipated, as had the burning desire to whip the phone against the wall. All in the past. He sat happy and cool and glowing while watching Del Rey's homerun in replay.

It was post-primetime when Steve heard the knock at the door. He knew right away who it was. Too late to be Jehovah Witnesses. Nobody but them ever knocked instead of pressing the doorbell. Nobody except Steve's son. And when he got up to answer the door, he ran through his mind all of the scenarios his only child could've gotten himself into.

Knocking and Steve flipped the switch to the porch light. He parted the blinds and saw his son grinning back at him. Hands in pockets, shoulders hunched. Steve closed the blinds, unlocked the door to open it. A chorus of insects greeted his welcome. Behind his son, to the left, a lightning bug blipped then disappeared. He looked back at his son. He blinked and smiled. Well into his twenties and wearing that smug skateboarder's smile: Rad man, rad. He was a proper fool.

Steve just offered a blank.

"Hey, Dad."

No answer. Only staring. The darkness hugged the porch, hugged his son until he couldn't help but grin. The silence was palpable and the darkness only made it roar loader.

"Aren't you going to ask me to come in?"

Smiling. Hands still fishing in his trousers. The insects buzzed, clothing the nakedness of silence.

"Sure," Steve said.

He opened the door. His son walked in, nervous and looking the place over. A leather jacket wrapped his shoulders in a darkness all its own. It looked shiny, almost wet. The blackness of the outside world had added a fresh coat of paint to it. A little rainbow tag hung from the zipper.

"So, what's up, Kevin?" Steve had his hand on the doorknob.

Arms up. "I've got nowhere to sleep."

"Again?"

"My roommate moved away unexpectedly, just like that." He snapped his fingers. "Not a word of notice or anything. He said he had something lined up in Austin.

Austin. Can you believe it? Who the hell has an urge to suddenly move to Austin?"

"Your roommate."

Kevin's hands dove back into his trousers. He shrugged.

Steve closed the door. He sighed, shaking his head while considering the grain in the floorboards beneath him.

"What about your . . . significant other?" Steve asked.

"We're on shaky ground right now. Had a pretty big fight."

"And so you can't stay there."

"That's right."

Steve sighed again. He walked past his son, into the kitchen. He called from around the corner. "You hungry?"

Kevin shrugged even though his dad wasn't there to see it. "Sure, I guess so."

Steve came back with the box of pizza. "Had a few slices left over. If I'd known you were coming, I would've ordered something other than pepperoni."

Kevin opened the box. "Dad, I haven't been a vegetarian for years."

"Thank God you at least came to your senses about that."

Steve sat down on the couch. The TV was on. It had been the whole time. Hadn't bothered to turn it off after the game. The Pirates had won, thanks to Del Rey. But that was in the past now.

"Thanks." Kevin took a bite from a slice.

"Don't mention it."

Into the living room. He looked at his father but his father watched the tube. He took another bite and walked over to the recliner in the corner.

"So . . . I was wondering . . ." Kevin wiped his mouth.

"What?" Steve didn't take his eyes from the screen.

"Well, you know I have nowhere to stay tonight. I was wondering if I could stay here."

Steve pulled his eyes from the screen, looked over at his son. "I thought that was decided."

"Well, yeah, thanks." He swallowed and cleared his throat. "But I was hoping maybe I could stay, you know, a couple of nights, just until I get a few things straightened out."

"You know my rules."

"Yeah, yeah, I know."

Steve stared at his son.

"I came alone, didn't I?" Kevin said.

Steve grunted and returned his attention to the TV.

"Thanks, Dad. Thanks a lot."

"Don't mention it."

Kevin plopped into the chair. The pizza box rested on his lap. He polished off the piece he'd been working on and dove back in for a second slice.

"What are you watching, anyway?" he asked.

"I don't know." Steve scratched at his chin. "Some sitcom. It's a new one. I forget its name."

Kevin ate his pizza, nodding.

"It's not very good," Steve said.

Kevin wiped his chin with a sleeve.

"The new ones aren't as good as the old ones." Steve reached for the remote. "They never are."

Kevin adjusted himself in the chair. He caught the pizza box before it could slide down his legs onto the floor.

"They're mostly black shows now." Steve flipped through the channels. "Wouldn't dare put someone like Archie Bunker on nowadays. Now he was funny."

Steve flipping through stations and Kevin noshing on a third slice of pepperoni pizza. Steve yawned. He stopped at the Weather Channel.

"Did you see who won the game today?" Kevin asked.

"Pirates." Steve watched the cities scroll up, waiting for their weather on the next day.

"What was the score?"

"Three to two." Steve stifled another yawn. "Del Rey hit a homerun."

Kevin swallowed. "Del Ray is awesome."

Steve continued to track the weather. The local forecast came on eventually and Steve was happy to discover that tomorrow promised to be a sunny day. He tossed the remote to his son, still stuffing his face full of pizza. The remote bounced off the arm of the chair, slid between the cushions. Steve stood up and yawned one final time.

"I'm going to bed," he said. "Shut the TV off when you're done."

Kevin nodded. "Goodnight."

"Goodnight."

Steve scratched his ass and walked toward the stairwell climbing to his bedroom. Kevin watched his father step onto the first two stairs. "Thanks again, Dad."

Steve stopped for a moment to glance at his son. He grunted then retreated into the darkness of the stairwell. All of his petty present worries would become that of the past as he laid his body on the bed, his head on the pillow.

PHLOGISTON

Steve met the new engineer for the first time inside the men's room at his workplace. He was sitting in a stall, applying the finishing wipes to a healthy shit when the bathroom door opened and closed. Footsteps approached his stall. Through the thin crack of his door, Steve could see a tall black figure make a quick ninety degrees before being supplanted by the cold gray metal barrier. The new engineer. He knew it had to be. Didn't have to see his face. There was only one black person in the whole company, of all the shops. So far as Steve was aware.

A few more wipes and Steve stood up, zipped his fly. A urinal flush beside him, beyond the gray wall. A sink turned on and Steve listened as the splashing sound of water filled the room. A small curse evidence that the black man had turned the knob too far. Had to be careful with that faucet. It was tricky, Steve knew from experience. A few drops of water had probably found their way to the engineer's pants; at his crotch, down the legs.

Steve kicked the lever. A mighty whoosh whisked away the shit and the heavier molecules of stink from the air. And what the vacuum couldn't claim spilled over the gray walls, squirming its way into the vents of lockers, the black skin of the engineer, the nostrils of any loiterer outside the false security of the men's room door. Steve was proud of his stink. He didn't mind sharing it with the rest of the world.

He opened the stall door and almost bumped into the engineer.

"Excuse me," Steve said. "I didn't see you there."

"No problem."

The black man smiled — white teeth in sharp contrast to dark skin. Steve almost expected the man's throat to be bobbing up and down uncontrollably, struggling with the heat from the colony of stars set in their neat rows. And the whiteness near-blinding. Steve wanted to ask him how he got his teeth so sparkling. But thankfully the man turned at the corner and carried his secret away with him, down past the rusted ranks of lockers on either side and out through the door. Steve now all alone, buckling his belt. The flame resistant jacket hung on the hook to the stall door. He pulled it on and trod after the ghost-heels of the dark man.

The engineer stood beside the plant manager, listening and nodding to the older man prattling on. But then he turned around in surprise when Steve pushed through the door. Turned back to the manager but he'd ceased talking and pointed in Steve's direction. Steve buttoned his jacket and was about to walk by when his boss motioned him over.

"Steve, how's it going?" the manager asked.

"All right," Steve said. "Can't complain."

"Good, good." The manager held his hand toward the engineer. "Steve, this is David King. He's our newest engineer."

Steve cuffed the sleeves to his jacket.

"David, this is Steve. He's one of our hot press operators." The manager smiled. "We keep him locked away in the backroom."

David turned to face Steve. "Nice to meet you, Steve."

"You too."

Steve offered his hand, but David just smiled. He looked past Steve and at the bathroom door he'd just come through. He ignored the handshake. Steve's pleasant smile soon dropped. So did his arm.

The manager coughed. "David's got a few ideas for the presses that might make the parts look better — even better than the ones the Japanese have on the market right now."

"Is that so?" Steve's mouth an I-beam on its side.

"And he should know." The manager grabbed the engineer's arm, pointing at him. "He's worked for the Japanese before. In Tokyo I believe, right?"

"Kyoto."

"Right, right." The manager stopped pointing but maintained his grip on the arm. "We'll have them on the run in no time, though, won't we? We'll be top dog again."

"Just a few changes in the process." David shrugged, looked at his feet.

"A few major changes," the manager said.

He patted David's arm but David just shrugged again.

"He'll be going over them with you and the other operators here soon." The manager finally released his grip. "But right now I'm just taking him around the shop, introducing him to those who haven't had a chance to meet him yet."

Steve's sheet metal face was uncreased — hadn't the ability to reflect light. His eyes dull flat marble.

"But pretty soon," the manager said, "things will be running quite a bit differently back there in the press room. Actually, in a couple other departments, too. But the press room will be hit the hardest."

David looked at Steve, put his hands behind his back.

Steve's blank face finally moved. It wrinkled. Corrugated metal over and between the eyes.

"I've been in my department for almost thirty years," he said. "I've seen a lot of you guys come and go, messing with the process, trying to make things better, but things never really change." Steve held David's gaze. He wouldn't look away for the world. Not for anything. "It'll just be a matter of time before your changes are forgotten and we're back to doing things the way they've always been done."

Steve left the two standing there. He went to the wash station to the side and stepped on the lever. Water sprayed in jets in the shape of an umbrella. His back turned to the two men, but he could still hear them. Some mumbling and then, "Let me introduce you to Carla in the OD department," from the manager. Steve heard them walk away. By the time he turned the handle on the paper towel dispenser, they were totally gone. Even out of earshot. Steve threw away a ball of towels before heading back to his department.

Warm and angry. Steve couldn't help but feel that way. He welcomed the familiar ringing sound his press faithfully emitted every second of every minute of every hour of every day for the last twenty-eight years. Steve trusted the unchanging ring, the sting of heat in his gloves, the cold metal surface of the cooling table. These things were familiar. These things were ever-present. And none of these things would get the company out of its slump any more than a fresh-faced post-ghetto engineer tinkering with the process. But at least these few constants were a comfort. Anything new, anything that could be a potential waste of time, was just plain annoying.

NIGGERS

That same day, at lunchtime, Steve and the guys sat around the break room table they always sat around. All of them eating, all of them drinking. And in between, sooty flowers of conversation would bloom.

"Did you guys see the new guy?" Ted said.

"How could you not?" Ozzie said. "He's blacker than sin."

"Straight from the fucking jungle," Ted said. He turned to Dave. "Did he come by grinding?"

Dave grunted in the affirmative. He bit into an apple.

"What about you, Steve? He come by your way?"

"I didn't see him back in the presses." Steve hadn't looked up from his magazine.

"He came back there," Donnie said. "I saw him. He seemed nice."

Steve turned a page. "He's a dickhead."

Ted leaned in. "Where'd you see him."

"Fucking pompous prick," Steve said. "Met him outside the bathroom." Steve finally looked up. "He wouldn't shake my hand."

"Why not?" Ted asked.

Dave looked at Steve with the apple in his mouth.

Steve shrugged. "I don't know why, they're all the same. You try and figure out why they do anything the way they do."

"What? Because he's an engineer?" Donnie asked.

"Well, that, too." Steve buried his face back into the article he'd been reading. "They make more money and don't get dirty and went to some goddamn college so they're so much smarter than the rest of us. I bet he doesn't know the first thing about turning a wrench."

"That and because he's black," Ted said. "They're

49

lazy bastards, got lazy work ethics."

"Fucking niggers," Ozzie said.

Dave nodding while crushing the apple to pulp between yellowed teeth.

"And because he's one of them that happened to make it, that's making a decent living, he thinks he's risen so far above the blue-collar white man that he can't even shake our hand." Steve flipped another page. He wasn't even reading it now. "What's wrong with my hand? What, do I have AIDS or something?" Steve held up his hand for inspection. "Look at it. Do you see anything wrong with it? Is it dirty, scabby, got shit all over it?"

Dave and Ted and Ozzie grunted and shook their heads and said, "No, no."

"He shook my hand," Donnie said.

The guys turned to him.

"That's because you're a nigger lover," Ozzie said.

The guys laughed.

"Whatever, man," Donnie said. "I just think that you're being a little hard on him."

"Look here." Steve stared into Donnie's face. "The fucking guy wouldn't shake my hand. Now I don't care if he's white or black or purple or fucking plaid, he wouldn't shake my hand. That's all I need to know about him. He's a fucking dickhead."

"Goddamn niggers," Ozzie said. "They're all the same."

Dave grunted and tossed his apple core into the garbage can.

Ted nodding. "You can't trust them, and you can't count on them for anything."

"You guys are racists, you know that?" Donnie snagged the newspaper from a nearby table.

"So what if I am," Ozzie said. "At least I'm honest about it."

"What the hell's that supposed to mean?" Donnie had paused; hadn't quite opened the paper yet.

Ted cut off Ozzie from replying. "I think what he means is that we see what we see and don't try to candy-coat the reality. Ozzie and I, and even Steve, too—we've all worked with black people before. I've known very few who were really worth a damn, very few who could pull their own weight and not fuck off all the time." Ted now leaned in toward Donnie. "You know what I'm saying?"

"Yeah, that you're a racist, too." Donnie opened the paper, tried to read it.

Ted shook his head. "You young guys, you're all the same. You've got easy solutions for a world full of mistakes and complications. You've got no real wisdom—haven't been around long enough to know what I'm talking about."

"My son's like that, too," Steve said. "Thinks he knows how the universe runs but doesn't really now dick. I mean, he never listens to a goddamn thing I say."

"Yeah, we've been around," Ozzie said. "We know what we're talking about."

Donnie looked up from the paper. "Jesus, Ozzie, you're only five years older than I am. I doubt that there are many life experiences you can pass on to me."

"I've got a kid," Ozzie said. "Have to take care of him, clothe him, feed him, wipe his goddamn ass. There's a lot you can learn from me."

"I already know how to wipe my own ass." Donnie folded the paper with a loud snap and began to read.

The guys laughed.

Ozzie just said, "Fuck you, Donnie," and kept his fuming to himself.

Once the laughter had died off, Ted said, "You'll see what we're saying when you have to deal with one of them. They'll be all nice and everything's going fine until one day you're not looking and they stab you in the back."

Steve pointed a finger at Donnie in support of Ted's statement. He'd closed his magazine and pushed it away from him, an inch from Dave's grasp, but he just grunted and ignored it.

"I dated a black woman once," Donnie said. He ignored their stares and kept reading.

Dave continued to ignore the magazine.

Ted's mouth hung open.

Steve slowly ground his teeth to pebbles.

"I think I'm sitting at the wrong table," Ozzie said.

Steve turned from Donnie to Dave. "I heard that Bev Campbell has a daughter who was married to a black man. She's got black grandchildren."

Dave smiled with a grunt.

"Who's that?" Ozzie asked.

"That fat bitch in inspection on second shift," Ted said. "She's got blonde hair—always has a ponytail."

"Oh, yeah." Ozzie tapped on the table. "I know who you're talking about. She's a cow, isn't she?"

"She's a goddamn house," Steve said, arms outspread. "And she's got fat little black brats running all over the place like mice."

"Probably on welfare," Ted said.

"And they're going to grow up and put their kids on welfare," Steve said. "And on and on down the line until the government wises up."

"Fucking leeches." Ozzie folded his arms and leaned back in disgust.

"I bet that makes quite a family portrait," Ted said.

Steve busted out laughing. Even Dave couldn't contain himself.

"Imagine that." Ted's grin spread broad and red. "All of them lined up in a row like swans." Ted laughed. "And then you come across a couple of ducks."

"Black mallards," Steve said. Almost crying he was laughing so hard.

"A couple of ugly ducklings." Ted rocked by spasms.

"You guys could learn some tolerance," Donnie said, reading the paper, refusing to look up.

"Family portrait," Steve said. "That's a good one."

Dave was grunting so hard and fast that the guys almost expected his chest to burst.

"Ugly fucking ducklings," Ozzie said, shaking in his chair.

"They're like Oreos." Steve held his gut. "They've got the chocolate cookies and the cream filling."

"And they're—" Ted tore his head from the table. "And they're double-stuffed!"

Ted's head dropped back to the table and the guys were lost in fits of laughter.

"Fucking niggers," Ozzie said.

And Donnie just shook his head, unsmiling, and read the paper.

Steve didn't have his daily beer inside the truck. He decided to drink at the bar instead. He needed to be around people, to see familiar faces, at least for a little while. A little reassurance. A little simplicity. He still felt the taint from his unpleasant experience with the new engineer. Familiar faces, reassurances; they would help wash away the bitter sense of foreign infestation in his brain. Steve knew the engineer would be there for a while. He knew he'd last. That kind always did. Just loved posing as the big cheese in a small, rural shit-town factory. Steve only hoped that it wouldn't take long before the easy pace of the coffee-wielding shop workers rubbed off on him. And they just installed a brand new air conditioning system. Maybe that would help cool him down.

But Steve was through with speculating for now. He just wanted to immerse himself into the familiar sink and settling of his favorite bar. A cold draught. Maybe two. An extra one wouldn't hurt. He needed to soak the taint, anyway. Wash it in the smells of ordinary things.

Steve parked beside the sign. It towered over him, shading him from the sun. Paint peeled from its poles. There was a crack in the wood, through the name: The Station. A meeting place for the everyday people to come to talk about everyday happenings. A common watering hole. A resting spot along the tarred expanse in the time between the first and second halves of the day.

A familiar creak and slam and Steve was through the door. It was busy. Always was this time of day. Some guy from the side, half out of a booth, yelled to him. Steve nodded, held up his hand. He approached the bar, squeezing himself between two guys on stools facing away from each other.

"Hey, Steve," the bartender said. "How's it going?"

"OK, Steph. How about yourself?"

Her arms bunched up as she looked around the room. "The same, as always." Then an index finger to a customer at the end of the bar. "I'll be right there."

Steve liked Steph's shirt. More importantly, he liked the shapes of what was held within her shirt. Couldn't help staring.

"So what'll it be, Steve?"

He snapped his head up. "Coors Light."

"Still drinking light?"

Steve shrugged.

She grabbed his mug from the rotating rack behind her. Number twenty-eight. She angled the glass under the tap and pulled on the lever.

"Got to keep my girlish figure somehow," he said.

The guy to Steve's left looked over his shoulder. "If that's a girlish figure, then your tits must've slipped down to your stomach."

Steve laughed. "Hey, Doug, I didn't see you sitting there."

"Sure, sure," Doug said. "You're just too good to associate with people like me."

"You've got a point there. Guess I'll have to find someone more respectable to talk with."

Doug laughed and slapped Steve on the back. "So how've things been going?"

"All right, you know, the same old same old."

Doug nodding. "And work?"

Steve shook his head. "I'd rather not talk about work. Wouldn't want to bore you with that shit." He reached for his mug. "Thanks, Steph."

But she'd already gone, tending to the clump of guys huddled around an empty pitcher at the end of the bar.

"Well, good for you," Doug said. "Leave work at work and drink when it's time to drink, I say."

Doug raised his mug and Steve raised his as well. They clanked glass and each took a healthy drink. Steve pulled his mug away with a sigh. He was transfixed by the little metal tab stuck on the glass with the twenty-eight etched into it.

"Boy, I wish I was twenty-eight again," he said. His mug high up in the air.

"Don't we all?"

Steve took another sip and slowly spun around to ogle Steph from a bar-length away. She washed glasses in the sink under the counter and nodded at something someone said. Her tits bounced. Two water balloons a prick away from bursting.

"Yeah, if I was twenty-eight again," Steve said, "I'd try everything I could to get my hands around that."

Doug shook his head. "Christ, Steve, she's just a kid."

"Yeah, I know that." Steve turned to Doug. "I'm just saying if I was twenty-eight again, you know?" He took a sip.

"You old fucking dog." Doug swiveled to the guy

beside him. "Jim, this old goat here is Steve. We used to party a lot when we were younger."

Steve shrugged.

"And this is Jim," Doug said. "He works with me at Mold Tech."

"Yeah, I think I've seen you in here before," Jim said.

Steve hugged his mug against his chest. "Well, you know, I pop in here every now and then."

"This one here's a horn dog. A goddamn pedophile." Doug's head bobbed at Steve. "You better keep a tight leash on your daughter or Steve here just might gobble her up."

"Like hell," Steve said.

Doug laughed and drank his beer. Jim ran a finger down the side of his mug. Steve sneaked a glance over at Steph, heading back to his end of the bar. He polished off his beer.

"Hey, Steph," he said. "Can I get another one of these?"

"Sure."

She grabbed his mug and refilled it while glancing from the tap to the customers in the bar. Steve watched her work until his old buddy Doug spoke.

"Well, it's good seeing you out again, Steve. Been a while."

"Yeah, good to see you, too. We'll have to get together sometime."

"Like in the old days." Doug winked.

Steve chuckled. "Not quite, can't keep up anymore. But maybe we could drink a couple watching Pittsburgh stumble through a game at my house."

"Sure, sounds good."

"Here you go, Steve," Steph said.

Foam ran down the side of the mug onto the countertop. Steve threw down a couple of bucks and grabbed his beer. She scooped up the money, rung up the register, slapped the spare change into a beer ring and finally turned to retrieve a bar rag.

"See you around," Steve said to Doug.

Doug had been talking to his friend Jim. He looked over his shoulder with a smile. "You're not leaving now?"

"After this beer."

"All right." Doug waved his mug at Steve. "You stay out of trouble, now."

"Nice meeting you," Jim said.

Steve nodded but his attention was glued to Steph's chest as she wiped the counter down. "Watch your glass," she said to a customer and then wiped the rest of the green Formica before dropping the soaked rag out of sight. She glanced up at Steve but he'd suddenly become interested in a black and yellow ad for Crikey's Hard Lemonade pinned to the side wall. Steph resumed her work and Steve wondered who the hell would want to drink lemonade in a bar. His focus slipped an inch to a bitter face pressed up against dark paneling. The man scowled at Steve; his hand on a glass of beer resting on the bar. Maybe it kept him anchored. If he'd bother to whip the glass across the room at Steve's head, he'd probably sink to the floor in a jumbled heap. Piss ass drunk. And he looked angry enough to make such an attempt. Steve just acted like he didn't see him and took a real slow drag from his beer. Steve's eyes shifted again to the Crikey's poster: When life gives you lemons . . .

"You see that guy down there?"

Bones Jones had crept up to Steve without him noticing. One of the local drunks. He was always here, but this wasn't one of the familiar faces Steve had hoped to meet. The man was grime. From the tight dirty curls of his head to the smudged cheeks with the sparse brown beard down a filthy chicken neck into a stained blue mechanic's shirt with rolled-up sleeves revealing a messy network of hair and freckles spreading into his hand with fingers clasped around a bottle of Crikey's Hard Lemonade ending in thick, untrimmed fingernails of dirt and condensation just beyond the peeling label. And he was tall. Tall enough to collect the dust from ceiling fans, inflatable beer blimps and dirty gossip.

"Huh?"

"That guy right there," Bones Jones said, pointing at the guy propped against the back wall. A black, greasy vein stopped just short of a knuckle.

"Yeah, I see him."

But Steve wasn't looking at him. He was afraid that Bones Jones's finger would push the scowling man's button and bring a heavy glass bomb on his head.

Bones Jones smiled. More black spaces than teeth. Whether missing or coated with motor oil, Steve could never tell.

"He's crazy," Bones Jones said.

"Oh yeah?" Steve tried to sound like he didn't care. He swallowed a cold, hard lump of beer.

"Oh yeah." A bony finger dug into the tangled forest of his cheek. "He'd kill everyone if he had his way. That's what he told me."

Steve nodded and waited for the sound of smashing glass.

"Guess he just doesn't like people." Bones Jones withdrew his finger and analyzed any accumulation.

"He looks crazy enough," Steve said.

"Don't tell him, though." Bones Jones stabbed the air with his finger. "It'll set him off."

Steve suppressed a shudder. "Looks like he's about to go off right now."

And it was true. The scowling man's face was red and bloated with rage. Steve could almost hear the man's glass begin to crack beneath an iron grip.

Bones Jones smiled again. "Oh no, he's fine now, he's not mad." He stooped closer to Steve's ear. "Just don't let him hear you call him crazy."

Steve's eyebrows lifted. "Yeah, well . . ."

Bones Jones tipped back his bottle. He didn't let up until all of it was gone. Steve was surprised that the man didn't swallow the damn thing whole. His eyes lit up suddenly.

"They're playing my songs now," he said. "You like Supertramp?"

Steve shrugged.

Bones Jones sang. "Right, right. You're bloody well right. You got a bloody right to sayyyyy."

He spun, carried his lanky frame to the bar and slammed down the empty bottle.

Steve didn't bother saying goodbye and he definitely didn't bother turning around to check up on the scowling man. Maybe the guy had given himself a stroke or something. The world, or at the very least this bar, would be a safer place. He walked into the next room to talk briefly to his friend who'd waved to him when he'd first entered. And while in the room, talking and drinking, he was thinking the whole time how much he wanted out of the place. He could feel the angry man's stare—could feel his desire to sink eyeteeth into the back of Steve's neck. And Bones Jones still singing at the top of his lungs: "You got a bloody right to sayyyyy." Steve knew that the bartender's eyes must've been rolling. Whose wouldn't? Even Steve had to catch himself lest the friend he talked to think he disbelieved every word.

Eventually, gratefully, Steve was ready to leave. He'd finished his beer and was about to take it up to the bar when he saw Bones Jones smile his broken-tooth smile at him. He knew another conversation would be inevitable, so he just left the mug sitting on a table to the left of the door. A quick glance at Steph, but her back was turned and he couldn't see her ass. So then the black and yellow sign's advice: When life gives you lemons . . . drink Crikey's Hard Lemonade. And of course the man scowled at him. He'd finished his beer, too, and was rolling the mug between his palms. Gearing up for something. Steve didn't want to know what.

He pushed through the doors that creaked, always creaked, but even this familiarity failed to do a damn thing for him.

Steve sat on his couch with a copy of Field & Stream propped against his crossed legs. An article on fishing for bass in the early Fall. Steve had the fan set on high, blowing stagnant air, rippling the pages. It was the middle of August and hot enough for him to lounge about without a shirt. Gray chest hairs glistened with sweat. Sometimes a bead would roll down the bulge of his midsection and fall into the black hole belly button. Or else moisten the waist of his denim shorts. It didn't matter where it ended up. His whole body was slick with perspiration. The rolling sweat felt like crawling bugs. Sometimes he'd slap himself. Then he'd allow the slip back into the autumn world on the pivoted pages stuck against the damp skin of his legs.

Autumn — real Autumn, post Indian Summer — was at least a couple of months away. But Steve liked to be prepared for the fishing season. And he loved the autumn winds, the autumn smells — the crackles, silence and overcast skies. He loved them all. And even if the Field & Stream in his lap was a few years old, the same situations always presented themselves, year after year, and this magazine offered the best advice. The same solutions. Familiarity. Sights, smells and motions. Year after year. And that was all right by Steve.

Pictures of Fall foliage and a grinning man in a boat. He knew bass swam in deep water during the Summer. But as the temperature changes, the water cools and the bass move into shallower areas. They come up from the depths to the surface. And that's why the man in the boat was always smiling. It was always Fall in his world and the bass were always coming up from the depths. And the nice guy was just passing this information along to Steve. But Steve already knew all about it. But it gave him comfort all the same.

Then a fly landed on his chest and crawled down in a hurry toward the bloated white hill. Steve swiped at it before it could seek to hide in the navel. He pulled his hand away. Wetness on the tip of his finger. He put it in his mouth. Only the taste of salt. No squashed bug tang. Maybe the fly escaped. Or maybe it had been just a drop of sweat. Steve unstuck the magazine from his leg and flipped it over to the opposite page.

Not a soul in the picture. Just the leaf-covered landscape jutting out into a wide stretch of water. Some lake in Vermont or Pennsylvania. It didn't say. But Steve knew the bass were there, at the sandy shores and the blunt rocky faces sticking up from the water. At the edges of weeds the little beasts would lurk. Ready to feed on the smaller fish. Watching and waiting at the surface. Unknowing that they themselves were being watched.

Steve felt an itch in the middle of his back. He worked his shoulders against the fabric of the couch, but he couldn't seem to get at it. He sighed and uncrossed his legs, leaning forward with the magazine in one hand. Fingers couldn't reach it either, so he folded up the magazine and rubbed the edge of it down his back. The fan agitated him further, blowing against the sweat, cooling it down, making it itch. He scratched madly at his chest with both hands and soon forgot about the itch on his back. He pushed back against the couch's rough surface, feeling a little relieved, and peeled the damp paper from his belly. The smiling man in the boat. He'd already seen that. He turned the page, pressing the article out flat, smoothing the wrinkles from the fan's constant wind.

In the Fall, shad start to roam about in the big lakes. Bass eat shad. They may react to these migrations and follow them closer to the surface, especially in areas thick with vegetation. At these moments they're most vulnerable, aside from being beached. This is when the boatman lands his quarry. Steve did the same. All it took was patience. He sat in the boat, too, waiting for the school of shad, watching for any breaking bass. He had a rod equipped with the appropriate lure: a lipless crankbait or some surface lure. And he always used the shiniest ones he had. The bass so often suckered by the glittering surface of metal. They were no match for the boatman. They were no match for Steve.

The phone rang.

"Goddamn it."

Steve slapped the magazine down on a cushion. He glanced at the clock: 10:30. People should've known not to call this late. He needed the time to cool down before bed. Steve sighed and heaved himself up on tingling legs. Waited a bit to let the sensation recede—become numb. Then wobbling to the phone in the dining room.

"Yeah."

"Steve, it's Joan. Is Kevin there?"

"No."

"Do you know where he is?"

"No." Steve tried to scratch at his back again. The itch had returned in force.

"You haven't seen him anywhere?"

"He hasn't been around in . . . I don't know, I'd say a month and a half." He leaned against the edge of the alcove separating the living room from the dining room.

"Well, I'm really worried about him. We had a fight a couple of nights ago and he hasn't been home since."

"Sorry, can't help you." Steve sliding up and down the wall's edge. "Wish I could."

"Well, if you see him, would you please let me know?"

"Yeah, sure." He couldn't get the itch.

"Thanks. Thanks a lot, Steve."

"Sure, but hey."

"Yeah?"

"Try not to call so late next time. I was winding down for sleep."

"I wouldn't have called if it wasn't important."

"Yeah, yeah, I know." Steve wiped sweat from his eyes. He was out of the fan's range. "But you could've called earlier."

"Don't give me that crap, Steve. You're probably sitting around in your underwear reading how to properly gut an elk."

"No, I'm not."

"Whatever, then. You'll call me if you hear from Kevin?"

"Yeah, yeah, I already said I would."

"All right. Goodbye."

"Bye."

Steve switched off the phone and scratched frantically between his shoulders with the stubby rubber antennae. A sigh of relief and Steve plunked the phone back into the machine. Then back to the couch, to the fan, to the magazine making constant flapping noises. He wiped sweat from his forehead and rubbed it on his shorts before dropping onto the soft cushions of the couch. Memories of Joan pushed from his mind. His son wasn't there. And Autumn only a few moments away. He picked up the magazine, closing his eyes to feel the breeze whip at the hair on his chest. He didn't even need to read the rest of the article. He opened his eyes and it was Autumn again.

When the wind picks up from the changing seasons, it glides along the surface of the water, super-oxygenating it. The wind also helps pile up the plankton, in time drawing the shad and ultimately the bass. Steve knew to fish in the areas where the shores were buffeted by the wind. More plankton would pile up. More shad. More bass. Steve fixing a minnow plug on his line. Only a matter of time before he caught one. All he had to do was watch and wait. The wind blew through his hair and Steve smiled in a boat on a lake.

It had started raining after Steve went to bed and didn't let up until the early morning. Fat drops still fell, but only in patches here and there. Steve wore a baseball cap to his truck in the backyard just in case it started to pour again. And the sky looked about to let go at any moment. Maybe if Steve sneezed . . .

The ground was wet. The air was wet. The trees, the bushes, the little chipmunks and squirrels all soaked through. Even the blackbirds hopping in search for flooded-out worms appeared slick with freshly dumped oil. Everything was wet. Steve trudged through the grass; his every step accompanied by a dull squish, giving him the impression of walking on the backs of waterlogged toads.

His neighbor burned his trash. Certainly far too early for it. And on such a rainy day. The guy still in his robe; some cheap fuzzy number most likely acquired from the clearance rack at Value City. Gaudy rainbow stripes ran down its length. An orange nylon rope wrapped around his middle. Black socks poked out from the tan uppers of work boots. A week's worth of beard growth dirtied his face. Steve planned on walking by, pretending not to see him, but the guy pulled his hand out of the barrel, looked up and waved. Steve waved back. The guy had a lighter in his hand. He stuck his fist back into the barrel and frowned into the rusted depths. And the rusted car behind him. That piece of shit Camaro still up on blocks. Probably always would be until it rusted completely through and some wintry gale scattered its uselessness all over a snowy lawn.

The squishes underfoot finally gave way to grates and slides. A large branch lay in the gravel beside his truck. He inspected the panels, the bed. There weren't any scratches or dents. Apparently it had missed, but not by much. He pulled the branch into the lawn and dropped it. A soft, wet thud and Steve squished his way back to the truck, looking down, scanning the driveway for any more obstructions. By his front tire, a few pebbles away from crushing tread, merciless rubber, a long, bloated worm slowly crept. A living length of snot, inching from the truck's shadow. Steve bent down to watch it. Then a flash of black to the side and he pulled his head up to see a crow flutter into the air. Another took its place, alighting on the soaked grass, hopping toward the truck, stopping then hopping again. The worm would be done for before long. Too exposed. Steve picked it up and flipped it where he'd dropped the branch. The crow flew away at the motion, eventually perching at the apex of an evergreen to await the departure of the human in his big metal box. Steve obliged. He hopped into his truck, started it and pulled out of the driveway. The worm would have to fend for itself. The natural order of things would continue, as it must.

And of course the dog on his rusted-out barrel. The natural order of things for Steve as he watched this little everyday reminder pass outside his truck's windows. It barked and barked and never stopped until Steve lost sight of him in the mirror as he turned down the street.

Then a sudden hail of bullets spattered across his windshield. He turned the wipers on high and leaned forward to try and peer through the clear spots. It was really coming down now. The waterlogged toads rained all around him. No longer underfoot. The thuds came on and on, steady and strong, while Steve blinked between wiper swipes. Then the red flash of brake lights and he eased onto the brake pedal. The rain was a bit heavier than normal, but still manageable. Steve could still factor it into the everyday. No reason to stomp on the brakes. Let the person in front of him wear out theirs. Wear out their vehicle, their nerves. Steve slowed then stopped, thumping the steering wheel with his thumb until the car ahead moved. He glanced at his clock. Plenty of time to get to work. No rush, no worry. The natural order still being played out.

He started moving and the rain stopped. In an instant. The turning off of the sky-high sprinklers and Steve watched everything around him drip. Trees, houses, cars, people. He flipped his wipers to intermittent. Tiny rivers slid from his roof down the windshield as he braked. And then thrown over the truck's edge by swiping rubber.

And there was the Paki out on his driveway, diverting the wash tumbling down the side of the street with a taped-up sweeper. He pushed it away from his driveway, saving his precious little gravel-children from the floods sent to wreck such unnatural perfection. Steve smiled. Of course the rocks were already drenched; the ground below them swelled, lifting them from their neatly raked beds. An exercise in utter futility. But the man tried yet to maintain some semblance of order with his pathetic broom. The natural order of things swept down the decline. Even if it was a stupid thing to do.

Steve traveled alongside the streams being swallowed and disgorged by the gutters. They collected in a vast lake at the bottom of the hill, but it could hardly be a match for his truck. The reservoir only came to the bottoms of his hubcaps. He plowed through the water with a roar and charged to work on the collective power of a lion's pride. It didn't rain at all the rest of the way and, when he finally walked through the double doors to his workplace, he knew he was just an extension of the street's rivers and that he'd arrived at his own appointed lake. The natural order of things had led him here and would lead him on through the rest of the day.

An hour before lunch that very same day, Steve was leaning against the wall in front of the console to his press, as usual, when Bob MacKenzie, who everyone called "Mac", approached him with a tape measure in his hand. He had a habit of pulling out the yellow strip a few inches before letting its metal tab slam his finger once the release button had been depressed. And he was doing it now. Pulling and retracting, pulling and retracting, over and over again. Steve turned when Mac stepped up beside him. And of course the relentless tape measure shuffle. Always the goddamn dance. Pulling and retracting when he walked, pulling and retracting when he talked. Steve bet the guy did it in his sleep until the worn metal casing slipped from his hand to the bedroom floor. Maybe the tape measure would still continue the dance of its own free will when its wheezing master had gone for good. Once he'd shuffled himself into the dark, lazy arms of death.

And it didn't look too far away. Mac looked bad. But then again, he'd always looked bad, as far as Steve could remember. Mac seemed old and unhealthy when he'd started twenty years ago and only slipped further into his ogre's hunch with each passing season. His belly, once the humble size and density of a bowling ball, had over time grown into a genuine boulder, weighing down his shoulders, the corners of his lips, the bags under his eyes. And hair! He'd once been clean-shaven and hidden all parts of his body under layers of flannel and denim. But now a forest dominated his face and neck and his persistence on wearing soiled tank-tops revealed that Mac had been more ape than human all along. His neck was once the size of a Sequoia; it was now thicker. His breath had stunk of beef stew and cabbage; now it just smelled of cabbage, only rotten to the core. Hands that had worked with certainty and care now fumbled with a tape measure. Feet that had lumbered with a lazy grace now moved to a chair to fall into or a wall to lean on. And now, too, resting his heavy shoulder to the wall that Steve had his back against.

"You know what I heard?"

But there were two things about Mac that never changed. For one, he loved spreading gossip, no matter how unlikely or damaging the juicy bits may've been. Maybe he never actually heard these rumors, but fabricated them instead, squeezing them from his hairy and shambling body with each labored step. Maybe they were only the gas that unconsciously crept from his orifices, through his pores.

Mac's hair was the second thing that never changed. Never even moved. Damp with Dippity-do, stacked in a thick black pompadour that challenged the ageless endurance of the great pyramids of Egypt. Everything else about his body sagged, drooped with gravity and decay. But not his hair. Not the shiny black obelisk. It demanded attention. The only element in Mac's haphazard body to do so. It even called insects to him. Gnats would buzz around the black monument. Mosquitoes would stab at it in the sacrilegious sport of seeking blood. Sometimes an errant fly would stick to its smooth, shiny surface. And stay there.

But he was a familiar face with familiar habits and Steve would be sorry to see him go. Even if he smiled like an idiot with a chunk of peanut wedged between yellow teeth and kept on pulling and retracting the damn tape measure.

"What's that, Mac?"

Mac didn't always expect snappy responses. His eyes shifted to the side. He slowly turned his head to scan behind him. Then back at Steve — pulling, retracting.

"You know that nigger that started here a little while back?" he asked.

"Yeah."

"Cathy said she saw him and his wife at the grocery store yesterday. At least that's what Cathy assumed she was."

"She didn't talk to him?"

"She said he pretended not to see her, just walked on by."

Steve didn't say anything. He waited for Mac to unload the awful burden of truth from his sagging shoulders.

Mac glanced behind him again. "He beats his wife."

"Oh yeah? And how do you know that?"

Mac leaned in. "Cathy said she had a black eye, how else'd she get it?" He smiled and flashed Steve the peanut. "Falling down the stairs?"

Steve shrugged.

"She said they didn't look very happy, either," Mac said. "Like they just got done arguing or something."

"Well, that doesn't surprise me really." Steve glanced at the clock on his console.

"Well, hell no, doesn't surprise anyone." Pulling, retracting the tape. "Just thought you'd like to know."

Steve nodded.

"Have you seen him?" Mac asked.

Steve nodded again.

"He's a big fucker."

"That he is." Steve looked past Mac, over his head, several hundred feet to the end of the department. "Stuart's looking this way."

"Let him look," Mac said. "I don't give a fuck what he thinks. What're they gonna do? Fire me for talking?"

"He's coming this way."

"Fuck him, the nosy bastard." Mac stopped his tape measure dance to cough. "I'll just tell him its work related."

"Uh huh."

A couple of seconds went by and it looked like Mac was about to sweat. He began madly pulling at the tape. Steve waited for the black volcano on top of his head to melt.

"He still coming?"

Steve nodded.

Mac pushed himself from the wall. He wobbled side to side then back and forth in see-saw fashion. It seemed that gravity would win after all, that it would pull down the huge, hairy bulk into a twitching ball on the shop's concrete floor. The pompadour swayed with a tsunami's vengeance. Threatening to break. He caught himself, though. If he'd crumpled at that moment, he'd never get up. And Steve suspected Mac knew this. His arms out, steadying, and the shudders began to ebb. Mac's eyes roamed for a vacant chair to crash into.

"Well, I better get back to work," he said.

"Yeah."

He shambled on past Steve and the press, almost tripping over the taped snake of cables running from the console to the wall. His drooping eyes bulged and the corners of his lips drew into a ridiculous frown. He sputtered then righted himself before walking through the entrance leading to the next department. A piece of paper fell from somewhere beneath the soiled tank-top, but he was already gone, pulling and retracting into a sloppy disappearing act.

Steve noted the paper. A crumpled Payday wrapper. He could tell by the orange letters. But he didn't move a millimeter from his spot on the wall. The only muscles that worked were the ones necessary for him to turn his head to check the clock. And then came the plant manager. Steve didn't nod or twitch an eye. His head rolled back to the console and he waited, arms folded across his chest, for the last few seconds of the press's cycle.

A shadow covered the edge of the control panel. Steve refused to acknowledge it and soon was rewarded with the sharp boom of the hydraulics from the retracting ram. Steve picked up his pencil and marked the peak temperature on the press log sheet.

"Where's Mac at?"

Steve finally turned to the manager. "I don't know, he went around the corner."

"What did he want?"

Steve watched the machinery inside the press move on the monitors' black and white screens atop the console. "Just wanted to know if we had any high-temp silicone back here."

The manager chewed the inside of his cheek. "Uh huh."

Steve still leaning against the wall, arms folded, acknowledging only the movements of the press.

"He's been dicking around all day. Haven't seen him do a lick of work." The manager watching a die transfer on the screen.

Steve's eyebrows lifted.

The manager looking around. The screens, the press, Steve—none of these things paid the least bit of attention. All too preoccupied. With the movements, the pressing, the heating. But that's the way it was supposed to be. Everything running fine, operators busy. All part of the natural order of the shop.

And then he spotted the white wrapper on the floor. He walked over to it, scooped it up, threw it in the metal pail beside the console. He glanced at Steve but Steve only sniffed and watched the screens. The plant manager nodded curtly before spinning on his heels and walking off in the direction Mac had disappeared.

The power to the press emitted its high-pitched wail. Steve donned his mask, wrote down some numbers, strode to the wire rack to pull on his hot gloves. The cycle had begun anew and Steve was there to help it along.

Steve downtown at the Country Fair pumping gas into his truck. He felt pretty good, pretty mellow. Work had gone by with almost no snags and the beer he'd polished off in the shop parking lot had washed away any care, worry, carcinogens in a cool amber stream. Cars pulling in and out of spaces in front of the store, people jumping in and out of the cars. Steve watched the dollars and cents climb on the pump's display. The price of gas had been steady since the severe peak of three month's past. But Steve had long since factored in this small change. Not that much more money and it hadn't affected his life in any real way. The price of pop, though . . . that might never level off. Pretty soon he could fill his truck with Mountain Dew and feel the perfect prince, riding on the sweetest octane the market had to offer.

A flashy green Neon zipped into the only vacant pump on the lot. The one directly across from Steve. Three girls were belched from the car, all wearing tight-ass shorts and tank-tops or half tees or sports bras in primary colors. And all bouncing in little bunny hops around the car, around the only boy with shaggy sideburns and wide black sunglasses. His crooked smile matched his easy saunter. Two of the girls broke off and followed him to the convenience store, still hopping in circles around their boy-toy planet.

The gas approaching the ten-dollar mark. Plenty of time to gawk. But the girls had just disappeared, leaving Steve with nothing to look at. No eye candy, only eyesores. Worn-out cars, worn-out persons, peeling paint, faded signs to store fronts that edged the streets on the station's sides. All too familiar reminders that something new wasn't so bad after all. So long as it came in manageable doses.

A flash of fluorescent pink and tight denim shorts stretched even tighter as the girl that had stayed behind bent over to retrieve the gas cap she'd dropped to the hot asphalt. A rude clunk from the pump. The numbers had stopped rolling on the display. Steve was about to pull out the nozzle when he decided to sneak another peak at the pert little girl caught in the space between the pump and towel dispenser. She stood up. Steve sighed. Disappointed that she'd found the cap so soon. One smooth leg now propped up on the concrete island's ledge and Steve ran its length to the hemline bunched up against her inner thigh, creeping its way into her damp panties, her moist hole.

She flipped her hair and shot an errant glance over at Steve, but he'd already shifted his gaze to the gas pump read-out. He waited a few seconds, watching the display in a show of mock patience. Then the nozzle yanked out and slapped back home in its dirty little niche. Drips of gasoline ran down the panel of his truck. He grabbed some towels, the whole time stealing glances at the taut little beauty rocking her foot on the ledge. The gas wiped off now and the cap screwed into place. He caught the number on the pump's side and walked to the entrance. He turned back once. The girl squeezed the handle to the pump and stared back at Steve with the familiar dirty-old-man stare. He smiled, turned red and made his way through the door into air-conditioned safety.

Lines snaked to the mile-wide counter. One of the brightly, barely clad girls was in the belly of a twisted snake with the way-cool boy behind her. A couple of other fresh female sights, too, deposited here and there among the aisles, in the lines, loitering and eating by the tables to the side in the small dining area. A canary yellow honey in the back, peering through the glass door of a refrigerated case. One of the girls from the car. Sad to say, Steve couldn't see much of her body. Stacks of crackers and chips and Pop Tarts obscured her sweet little ass from meat-seeking vision.

Steve was thirsty. He wanted a soda. Just so happened the bent-over canary was in the same place Steve wanted to be. He strolled to the case, stopping beside her, snatching side-wise glances, rubbing his chin in exaggerated contemplation. Ass or soda, ass or soda. Ass, ass, ass.

The girl scooted over, scanning the next case from top to bottom. She opened the door, put her hand on the cold head of an ice tea bottle. Bottom lip bitten and then frowning before stuffing the bottle back in place, scooting over once again.

Maybe ice tea was more of what Steve wanted. He slid over and watched the reflection in the glass of the next case. Tea or tits or tea or tits. Tits, tits, tits.

Canary yellow expanding on the glass, reaching for the door, pulling it open to rip ruby-red grapefruit juice from its slot. The door closed and she turned. Steve was there of course, blocking her path with his dense, male body, grinning with fool's lips, just happy to be an obstruction. And the girl grinned back. A flip of the hair, a jerk of the head, gaze to the floor and pupils shrinking beneath thin, brown eyebrows.

"Excuse me," she said and then she almost giggled.

"Certainly," and Steve stepped aside to let her pass.

She smelled of flowers and honey and virginal sweat. It was all Steve could do to not follow her every swishing movement down the aisle. His throat wet and slick and he searched in the glass for her lithe body. A canary yellow splash, but then again, a lot of other colors were reflected an inch above the Pepsi bottles' cool plastic skin. A lot of other yellows, too, but only one that moved. It proved to be too much for him. He turned around and watched that tiny little frame sidle up to her tiny-titted friend in line with the way-cool boy and his detached expression, blank staring at the sub menu behind the cash register. The girls giggled and covered their lips and eventually the canary yellow honey spun to regard Steve with a crooked smile. Her friend sourfaced and mouthed something to the sweet, yellow bird and the way-cool boy laughed with sarcasm vibrating in his chords.

Steve turned around. He hadn't realized he'd moved so far to the right when checking out canary girl. Now in front of Pepsi and confused at the absence of Coke. Three cases to the left and he caught the red label with the signature white scrawl. He went to the case and opened the door, bypassing ice tea and juice and multi-flavored milks and waters. Bright yellows, pinks, oranges all in alien rows. But the fire engine red of the Coke was familiar, comforting. Steve pulled out a bottle, uncapped it and downed a good portion of the caramel liquid right there in the store.

Now that he had the sugar, he needed a salt to balance it out. His mouth craved meat, from the tip of his tongue to the worn crowns of his molars. A display of beef jerky stood at the end of the aisle across from the Coke. Steve was unconsciously caught in this balance. And the whole time scanning and rescanning the shelves for his favorite brand, but all he could find was the cheap, kippered shit. He picked two beef sticks instead and strolled to the counter, hoping to catch a final snapshot of the lovely teen's canary back and shoulders on the way. Or even better, the cute little ass in tan corduroy shorts. No such luck. Out of the store and Steve couldn't spot them through the giant front windows.

Old ladies and old men, trailer trash and their trashy children, loud-mouthed guys with chew and overweight girls with hoagies, everyday men and women as everyday as Steve himself. These were the people who surrounded him. The people who always surrounded him. And Steve didn't mind too awful much. They made him feel a part of what was going on. He understood his role in this small town, in this community. He knew his place. But he also knew that once in a while it was only fitting to scope out the ordinary environs in search of the rare beast, the white hart: the occasional teenie wet dream fantasy or tightly clad strumpet or honest-to-goodness goddess sullying her feet on the hot, dirty pavement of his oh-so-average town. He was a man, goddamnit! And it was only proper for a man to ogle, to mentally grope. For him to dream his lucid little daydreams in the spaces between the everyday motions. Like those caught between an everyday pump and towel dispenser. It was only human. And it helped him through the duller moments until he found his way home to his magazine and pizza and prime-time TV.

"Can I help you?"

And so Steve popped out of his daydream into reality as he paid the cashier for the gas, Coke and beef sticks, pushing out of the store, onto the lot where vehicles performed their fragile dance with humanity. Steel bumpers and sneaker-hungry tires. Pedestrians both sleepwalking and aware. The girls were gone, taking their flashy Neon and way-cool boy-toy with them. Steve's eyes roved the tarred wasteland. A car waited behind his truck for its turn at the pump. Steve wasn't too concerned. He'd get there when he'd get there. No point in rushing, so he took his time, watching for the bone crushing bumpers and the voracious rubber wheels.

A honk and Steve whipped his head to the right, but it wasn't for him. Some guy with glazed eyes stared open-mouthed while the honker shook his fist behind a thin wall of glass. And then in the corner of Steve's vision, a squat little man with a gas pump nozzle crammed up his nose. The man turned, still sniffing, and Steve recognized him as the guy who'd nearly been swallowed by an eighties car-beast. The one who got orgasmic bliss from smelling motor oil. But now it was gas. Steve smiled to see that the man's taste in petroleum wasn't obsessed solely with the crudest, the blackest of choices. The man opened his eyes and started. He scowled at Steve, but Steve was already looking away and soon hidden by gas pumps. He climbed into his truck and pulled out from under the overhang. A pause at the exit, waiting his chance to melt into the busy stream of traffic. He turned around and watched the squat man with the penchant for petrol fumes waddle to the entrance of the store. And still he scowled.

Soon a space opened up and Steve zipped onto the street. He headed toward the grocery store to purchase the items required for his supper. Air funneled through the windows rolled halfway down. The sky clear, the sun shining. Quite a change from the morning's downpour.

He halted beneath the stoplight's red circle. The gentle hum of his truck idling and the moderate swooshes of cars passing through the intersection helped set Steve at ease. He didn't mind waiting. It was his turn. Soon the colors would flip from red to green and he'd be on his way. But for now this pause was definitive. Necessary and serene. He uncapped his Coke and a quick flash of red preceded the gulps of soda.

CLASSIC.

The light turned green and Steve placed the bottle between his legs before taking a left. Not going to the store after all. Too nice of a day to sweat away in a cramped kitchen baking chicken pot pies. He'd go out to eat. And the idea made him smile. But of course he'd already been smiling from the smooth ride of his sleek red truck and the grace granted from a green circle, blessing his afternoon with the freedom to sail on past the sorry suckers stuck at the reds on either side.

ENJOY.

Steve entered the steakhouse. It was no different

from any of the others that dotted the country from East to West coast—from Canada to Mexico. The same sights, smells, restaurant help garbed in the same stone-washed jeans and polo shirts; the same fare in the same rustic menus with the same prices ranging from affordable to slightly obscene. And one of these cloned steakhouse workers seated Steve in the booth he always sat in, across the backs of two more booths where a large wagon wheel was spiked against the wall. Soon the waitress came and scuttled off to grab his Coke, leaving Steve to contemplate the reprints of Western posters and a vast assortment of wooden and cast-iron equipment from pioneering days. But Steve was no pioneer, he knew. Would've been one of those Yankees that came in after the Gold Rush to start his new job at the paper mill. So there was no special affinity with the bygone, pioneering spirit. Just used to the place. Maybe his ancestors, too, were used to the hot, dusty summers in creaking, wooden buildings that pounded trees to pulp and eventually to paper. But Steve hardly gave the joint so much consideration. His face in the menu. Already immersed in the thick slabs of grilled steaks, slipping in their juices, gliding along gravy streams.

His waitress caught him off guard when she'd returned with his Coke. She smiled, handed him the soda. Liquid dripped down the sides and so the glass slipped through his hand, slamming the tabletop before spilling into his lap. The waitress's smile had disappeared and Steve jumped from the bench, banging his knee against the table.

"Oh, oh, oh, I'm so sorry, sir."

She wiped the soda with the cloth napkin on the table, but they'd soon soaked through. To no effect, Steve swiped at his pants, watching the liquid fall from the booth onto the wood floor. The waitress scrambled around, apologizing, then darted toward the backroom saying, "I'll be back with a rag." Steve looked around the room, hoping no one had noticed, his hands up, wet and sticky and smelling of sugar. She came back with a small damp towel and squeegeed the cola off the seat onto the floor.

"I'll be in the bathroom," Steve said.

She made a sorry face and Steve split, striding across the dining area toward the restroom with his hands still in the air. He backed through the door, pivoted and walked to the sink to turn on the water. The hot water faucet was broken, of course, so he yanked on the other and, of course, it sprayed cold water all over his pants and shirt, splashing over porcelain, dark-spotting the bare concrete floor. And of course he swore the whole time. But then he'd quieted the deluge, pressed folded towels around his crotch and belly. It hardly seemed to work. A hand dryer mounted beside the towel dispenser. Steve moved to it and positioned the lower half of his body beneath the blasting furnace. And he kept wiping at himself, looking over his shoulder at the door, praying no one entered and got the awkward visual of Steve pulling at his crotch. And of course, someone did come in to hesitate a moment before pretending not to see Steve and disappear gratefully behind the metal wall of the restroom stall. Steve took this as his cue and slipped silently through the door into the hallway. His pants now both hot and cold. And unmistakably wet.

"I really must apologize," the waitress said. "Sometimes I'm so clumsy."

Steve sat himself on the dry bench of the booth.

"No, no, it's my fault," he said. "I didn't have a handle on it."

A fresh glass of Coke sat in front of him, the surface wiped clean of condensation. Steve sipped from it and nodded.

"I'll give you more time to decide what to order," she said.

"That's all right, I know what I want." Steve

peeled the menu from the table, pulled it open with a quick tearing sound.

"The menu's a little wet," she said.

"I see that." Nodding with a smile.

The waitress waited with hands behind her back. Her face wrinkled in concentration as Steve scoured the items for his preferred steak. "The Delmonico," he said and handed back the menu. She went through the side dishes, the trimmings, the salad with its short list of dressings. Every one of these answered and so she filled in her little pad and slipped away into the backroom. Steve watching her departure, sipping from his Coke. Of course he looked at her ass and anticipated her coming back so she could walk away again. Especially the walking away part.

An angry female voice punched through the silence. From the side, somewhere beyond the wooden barrier running the length of booths in which Steve happened to be sitting. He could only see the tops of other booths nestled against the far wall. A hushed masculine voice overpowered the female squeak and then eventually the silence returned. Steve raised himself a bit to peer at the tables on the other side. A few couples and one four-member family clustered in tiny corrals amid a wide stretch of prairie. He scanned the customers, found the voice, it belonging to a black man — the black engineer from his shop, no less. His dark face crinkled in what Steve took to be annoyance. He hadn't spotted Steve and he was grateful, plopping himself back into the hard, wooden bench.

His mind drifted. His hands clasped and the thumbs lightly banging together. The waitress appeared, bearing his salad in her hand. Steve hadn't noticed her until she was almost on top of him. "Oh," he said and, "Thank you," before sticking his fork into a big white chunk of iceberg lettuce. Hadn't seen her coming, but he certainly noticed her going, every second until the cruel

wooden barrier claimed her. The piece of lettuce found its
way into his mouth.

And then another gruff response smothering the
female complaint. Steve peered over the ledge again, but
nothing had changed. The same people in the same
clusters. The same tables and booths. The black engineer
still visible and plainly too engrossed to notice a fellow co-
worker like Steve, spying Kilroy with the eyes out
popping and nose all dangling. Steve was a lowly press
operator, after all. How high could he expect to rate? What
chance a glance? Then a waitress brought a couple of
salads and slid them into the booth where the black
engineer and his mysterious partner were sitting. Steve
dipped again. He finished the salad, pushed away the
plate and waited for the main course.

Hands clasped again, thumbs banging silently.
Two more couples were seated in Steve's section. One
couple directly to the side, the other at the far end, both
opening their menus and listening to the list of specials, in
their turn, spouted from the plump lips of waitresses too
cute not to watch. Happy distraction for Steve. A firm little
ass and the jostles, twitches, scribbles and bends. Then she
left and her ass with her and Steve banged his thumbs
over and again.

And staring off into nothing as well. Until a vision
of beauty floated by, glided by, into the woman's
restroom. His eyes widened, but she'd already vanished.
Hardly enough time to take it in. But Steve held on to the
image, replayed it over in his mind: the flowing white
dress, summer dress with blue flowers the size of
butterflies all over it; the tall, lithe frame; the sophisticated
tilt of her chin; the long strawberry blond hair that shined,
even in the dull restaurant's lights; the pale skin, milky
smooth along arms and legs, peeping beneath the swoosh
of the dress, painting the dainty toes, trying to hide the
worn leather sandals. Steve played it again. And yet again.
His thumbs resumed thumping, waiting for the beauty to

rematerialize. He'd forgotten all about his food. And the servers in tarnished bodies. Compared to the beauty of beauties.

And then the waitress waltzed in bearing a tray of plates and drinks. Steve's mouth instantly started watering and he licked his lips as his dinner was laid out before him. His hunger had almost completely dissolved, but now it returned with twice the voracity. He dug in and cut up and slathered down and burped up and dribbled out gravy from the corner of his mouth. So hungry. So hungry indeed that he didn't bother to watch the waitress walking away. What was an ass shaking in the distance compared to twelve ounces of juicy steak under knife and fork? The succulent meat, blood and sauce, salt and spices and red pink center. He was utterly lost.

But then found at sea. Halfway through his baked potato he saw the beauty again. Even more than mere sight. He absorbed her. The sweet smell of flowers in rain broke through the carnal thoughts and acts of ripping, rending, gnawing, swallowing. Quelling the beast in gentle rain, flower waves. Steve had dropped his fork and forced a half-chewed chunk of flesh down his throat. She turned the corner, flipping her hair, and Steve suddenly felt dirty and insignificant. And he didn't look at her tits, didn't look at her ass. He took in the whole sight of her. The boldness and the beauty and the grace in movement. Her hands that swept through the air to forgive the soiled masses. The kind of woman who kings would wage war over. The kind of woman who'd reduce those same kings to paupers in the effort. The kind of woman who'd bestow kisses on peasants and raise up new rulers in the old kings' stead. The kind of woman the average man would try and appear a little less average when blessed with her awesome presence. And of course Steve was one of these average men. He'd closed his mouth at her passing and even attempted to brush his bangs over the receding forehead with fingers that almost shook. Almost shook.

He was a man, after all. Had to keep it together.

When the waitress returned to check on Steve, he was slowly finishing off the rest of his dinner. He nodded to her and asked for another Coke, but he couldn't bring himself to gawk at her. In fact, he didn't even want to. The vision of beauty in the white summer dress had completely cleansed his mind. He didn't even want to finish the steak, but it would be a complete waste not to. And Steve couldn't let things go to waste. But when the waitress had gone, Steve's face was in his plate. The blood-red juices, the melted butter, the bits of potato stuck to the plate and fork. But he hardly saw these.

Once again, Steve snuck a peek over the wooden barrier. More couples now. Some of the previous ones had already left. The black engineer had his elbows propped on the table, fork in hand. His plate nearly clean and a smile full of the white teeth spread along his dark face. He couldn't find the beauty and knew that he'd missed her. He sunk back into his booth, hunched over his plate. The steak a heavy lump in his gut.

So now done with his meal. He pushed himself from the table, threw down a few ones, a few coins and headed to the cash register. A guy in front of him was using his MAC card. Steve looked at the walls, the restaurant staff, the customers at their tables and those sitting by the door, waiting to be seated. Finally he let his eyes wander to the booth that held the black engineer.

And that's when he saw her. The beauty. She hadn't left. She'd been there the whole time and Steve hadn't known it. He believed that he could've felt her presence anywhere without actually having had the benefit of seeing her, but he obviously was wrong. Way wrong. And there she was; the pale arms to her side, disappearing under the table, the slightly parted pink lips, the strawberry blond tresses spilling over her shoulders and almost into her plate. There she was, there she was . . . sitting in the same booth as that black engineer, eating and conversing and every now and then, smiling at him. It seemed they'd settled their differences, their minor disputes. He heard her laugh and then a dark arm thrust out of the booth into the affected American, Old Western air, maybe showing just how wide his feelings for her were. Or maybe describing the length of his penis. But of course, she'd already know that. She was the African bushman's mistress, wasn't she? Had to be. No other possibility. Unless . . . but there was no way in hell Steve could see her being his wife. His wife? No fucking way.

Steve looked away, then at the ground, finally at the guy signing a receipt at the register. Steve scratched the back of his neck, head down again. The cracks in the floor were normal. The worn spots, the stains, the gauges deep and shallow. All normal. All part of the natural existence of a wood floor. No matter how big the crack, no matter how terrible on a molecular level the rift may've been, it was all normal. Factorable. The natural existence. Natural. But if the floor should split apart North to South with a great crunching cry, that would be far from ordinary — cause for great alarm — wholly unnatural. The people wouldn't understand, couldn't possibly begin to understand even when sent sliding down the slanted levels onto the cold concrete below. With broken limbs and ribs and petitions to God. No one could consider such a cataclysmic rending to be normal, as part of the natural existence of a wood floor.

Mocha fingers across a white-chocolate arm. Steve could feel the unnaturalness of it. The black man had leaned in and given a peck on that bloodless cheek, that beautiful, pale, snow-white cheek. And so now dirtied, adulterated. The vision of beauty began to blur, to leak off its bleached skin and mingle with the crude oil, the darkness of a caressing hand. What would the jungles of Africa do with such an exotic creature?

And then she raised her sleeve to scratch at her arm. A big purple bruise right below the shoulder. She

84

made a frown and he lightly rubbed at it with a dark finger. She smiled and he shook his head and then she shook her head, too, until they both started laughing.

"Did you enjoy your meal, sir?"

Steve turned to face the clerk at the register. He pulled out his wallet and paid the bill. Before he left, he snagged a red and white mint from an overfilled dish to the side. He walked toward the door, sneaking one more glance at the contrasting couple. Oblivious to him and soon obstructed by the back of the booth and then a coat rack to seal the lid. Steve untwisted the wrapper and popped the mint into his mouth. He pushed through the door, clomped down a decline and then out another door onto the sidewalk that ran the entire building's perimeter. He followed this until he came to a corner.

"So she didn't have a black eye."

A woman rounded the corner just then and gave him a quick look. Steve just pretended he hadn't said anything at all and kept following the sidewalk around the building.

ÉLAN VITAL

Snow fell lightly on the red hood of his truck. The roads weren't too bad. Clear enough. Steve had just finished his shift; a half-day before the start of Christmas vacation. Some of the guys had said they were heading to the bar at the bottom of the hill, so Steve popped in for a quick beer. He showed his face, waved a little, nodded and wished coworkers Happy Holidays before getting into his truck to roll his way home. And along this route the Station glowed in warm neon. An invitation. So he made a hasty turn into the parking lot, slid into a parking space cockeyed. He cut the engine. Didn't plan on being long. Just an extra beer to start his four-day weekend and he'd be back on the road. The place wouldn't be busy anyway. Only a few cars bothered to sleep in the near-freezing cradles snuggled against the building and the tall wooden fence that defended teetotalers from the die-hard, liquored-up regulars.

Steve removed his work cap and replaced it with one that wasn't gray with graphite dust. He pulled out his wallet, opened it and swore at the only dollar bill wedged between receipts. Thought he'd had more. He leaned forward with a groan, sliding out the coin collector and retrieving fingersful of multi-valued change. A struggle stuffing the coins into his jeans, dropping the wallet in the process from his lap to the floorboards with a wet slap.

Another groan as he picked up the wallet, wiping the mud and water on the edge of his seat. The door opened and landing on the ground with a squish and spray. Some of it got on his jeans. He bent to wipe it off and closed the truck door before standing up. It didn't matter. Everybody's legs were sure to be splattered. The parking lot was totally covered. And only getting messier as an industrial plow scraped by, shoving minor avalanches of slush ten feet from his truck.

Steve blinked away snowflakes tangled in his lashes. They melted and dripped into his eyes so he blinked even more. He sloshed up to the bar, past the wooden beams to the portico, between the curbs curving in toward the entrance. A two-dimensional paper wreath taped to the door with a frosty bottle of MGD poking through its center. He pushed through the doors and heard sleigh bells ringing. Nailed along the top of the door. One brass ball on the end drooped, almost fully emancipated from a droll existence of red felt and monotone jingling. And then other noises hit Steve's ear. Bar noises. He craned his neck then pushed through another set of doors with a brand new set of jingling balls.

"Hey, you're letting the heat out!"

This from a guy Steve only vaguely knew. He couldn't even guess at a name. Maybe it started with a B. And the guy smiled with an expression full of stagnant red blood and splashes of whiskey. A rocks glass of brown, watery liquid clinking in hand, balanced on a leg, sitting in a stool facing the door with its jingles. Steve noted the pansy little stirrer in the guy's drink and smiled. He nodded to him and approached the bar and thank heavens and their flowing-haired golden boy on this eve of the eve of his birthday of birthdays because Stephanie was behind the counter, pulling a tap and shooting quick glances from the mug below it to Steve.

"Coors Light?" she asked.

"You know it."

She nodded then walked away to give the man at the end of the bar his beer. The guy who'd kill everyone if he could. And he glowered at Steve. Didn't even acknowledge his freshly filled mug. Just kept staring at Steve with eyes afire. Maybe Steve was full of bullet holes or neat little knife slits. Maybe his face caved in and left him to choke on his teeth. Maybe Steve's own liver, recently gutted and leaking excess alcohol and fear, was tied around his neck and swaying, hoping maybe at last to squeeze out one big fat jingle. Whatever the case, the images caught among the flames in the glowering man's eyes were sure to be bloody and brutal beyond any average bar rat's imagination.

He turned away in time to catch the bar maid pull a bottle from the cooler and place it under the bottle opener screwed into a wall.

"Wait a minute!" Steve said. "I want it in a mug."

"I'll put it in a mug for you," and then she popped the cap.

"No." Steve shook his head. "I mean I wanted it from the tap."

"The keg's kicked."

"What the hell you giving the little lady all the trouble for," the guy next to him said. The guy with the whiskey in his lap. He twirled the candy-ass straw and took a tiny sip. He smiled.

Steve shrugged and smiled back. "I'll take Busch, then."

"No, no, hold on a minute there, missy," the guy said, turning toward the bar. Stephanie had almost pitched the bottle. "If he ain't going to drink it, I will. Don't want to see it wasted."

She plunked it on the counter, grabbed a mug from the rack behind her. "Slumming it with the rest of the poor folks, huh?"

"Can't see letting a perfectly good beer go to waste," the guy next to Steve said.

"You get laid off or something?" Stephanie asked.

Steve shook his head. "No, just thought I had more money on me than I do is all."

"Be a goddamn shame." The guy beside him slammed down a good portion of the bottle, pulled back for a big gulp of air, smiled and began stirring his teensy-weensy pantywaist straw.

Soon he had his beer. He sipped from it, noted the electrical lights stapled along the ceiling, hanging down in symmetrical bows. He surveyed the rest of the decorations. Garland snaked across the paneling above a set of shuttered windows, plump globes of glass and frost hung from the garland, tiny specks of primary and secondary colors speckled the globes, the speckles transmitted from the electrical lights across the room and from those wrapped around the Christmas tree stuffed in a corner beside a trivia machine.

And then a loud, familiar voice singing.

"Give a little bit, give a little bit of your love to me."

Bones Jones in the billiards section, behind the table, holding his pool stick microphone and screaming Supertramp lyrics red-faced and sweating. He hadn't had his hair cut in a while. Stuck up in a white man's fro. His beard, too, had overgrown his face and threatened to join the hair on his head in the effort to engulf and overpower his brain. Steve half expected hibernating squirrels to awaken and poke their twitching noses from the curly jungle and gnaw on their hidden stash of acorns.

He turned around to stare at Stephanie's ass, but she had it parked on a stool, propped against a beer cooler, watching one of those shows where some great embarrassing secret is revealed and the studio audience goes, "Oh, my God!" as the panel shake their heads, tuck tails between legs; girls cry and plead with balled-up tissue, dabbing wet cheeks and noses with soggy, severed bunny tails as their male counterparts huff and puff, squishing damaged hearts and betrayed souls hanging invisible somewhere slightly above their eyes; all this while the host clutches the microphone to his chest then waves it around the crowd, his face alternating between expressions of concern, judgment and scorn to end in a phrase, "Well, yes, I think that's the thing we'd all really like to know." Steve would've rolled his eyes, but he buried his face in his beer instead.

"Send a smile and show you care." The girl sitting in the booth next to the pool table tugged at Bone Jones's heavy flannel, telling him that it was his turn to shoot, but he just kept on singing.

"Now how could you let a perfectly good beer like this go to waste, Steve?"

Surprised the guy knew his name. The bottle tipped back and drained. Eyes filled with remorseless tears. The guy smiled and stirred the drink in his lap.

"What are you drinking a little girl's drink for, anyway?" Steve asked.

The guy stopped stirring and held up his glass. "This has got more alcohol in it than that mule piss you're drinking right there."

"Who the hell you fooling." Steve pointed his mug at the little Girl Scout-sized drink. "That's fucking ice tea, you lightweight."

Guffaws and then clinking his glass against Steve's. "Then here's to piss and ice tea on the happiest holiday of the year."

"You really got a way with words."

And then both guys took a drink.

A slam at the end of the bar brought Steve's head around. There he was again. Only now he looked meaner, if that were possible. And his empty mug rested on the counter in front of him. Face crushed inward, hawking up bile of the most caustic constitution. Hawking it up so he could spew it all over the bar and melt everything to useless lumps. All in a Pompeii minute. And his scowl focused on Steve.

"Hey, buddy." The guy next to Steve. "What the hell's your problem?" He stabbed the ice cubes in his drink with the little red straw. He wasn't smiling and the cranberry splashes on his face had darkened to mulberry.

Scowling man raised his finger and pointed past Steve's head. "I've got no beef with you." His eyes didn't waver once. Kept them clamped on Steve.

The deep red blotches slowly subsided, leaving only faint traces of anger in jagged streaks. Maybe it was just the alcohol. "Well, all right then." He sipped from his girly straw. "Just relax a bit, man.'

"Give a little bit, give a little bit of your love to me." The song was already over, but Bones Jones kept on singing. He knocked a few balls in the pockets. Some of them his own.

Steve drank his beer. Almost done with it. But he didn't want to rush himself. Didn't want to give the guy at the end of the bar the satisfaction of hurrying through his beer. He knew the guy was still staring at him, but Steve just set the mug down and watched the lights against the back wall blink in uncertain patterns. He wasn't going to hurry. No way. Maybe a bit nervous, but he wasn't a pussy.

"Hey, Steph," the guy next to Steve said. "Get that guy down the end of the bar another beer on me." He turned back to look at the guy. "Looks like he needs to loosen up a bit."

Angry man still shooting his scathing glare at Steve. And Steve, of course, continued to ignore him, devoting all of his attention to the lights, following their sequence down the line, along the wall, until he came to a poster of a redhead in a bikini holding a bottle of Killian's: Try a cold red one.

"Jesus, buddy," the guy went on, "it's Christmas. Time for good cheer, good will toward man and all that shit." He shrugged when angry man didn't answer. "Just drink up and you'll see." He glanced back at Stephanie who was nearly done pouring angry man's beer. "Why don't you give one to Steve here, too. He's been milking that thing forever." He leaned in to Steve. "Need a nipple for that thing?"

Steve waved his hand. "No, Steph, I don't need another one."

"Ah, come on, man." The guy rocked back in his chair, looking hurt, but Steve knew him for a drunk and bad actor. "It's fucking Christmas."

"I just don't want another one."

The guy looked all around, swiveling in his stool. "What the hell's wrong with everyone around here? Doesn't anyone want a free beer?"

Bones Jones jumped up from a crouch over the table. "Hey, hey! I'll take one."

"Well, all right, then." The guy beaming. "Give him one, too."

Stephanie looked over at Steve's mug and then at him.

"Someone's got to spread the Christmas spirit," the guy said. He swung back around to gawk at Stephanie's tits.

"What'll it be, Steve?" she asked.

The guy faced Steve with both arms out to his sides.

Steve looked from him to Stephanie and finally at his empty mug.

"All right, all right, I'll take another one," he said.

"There you go." Reaching out, patting Steve on the back.

Stephanie grabbed his mug and started filling. Then a dark, lanky shape in the peripheral caused Steve to shift his gaze. Bones Jones grinning and dancing in place, holding his mug out for Stephanie to refill. Beer caught in the tangled mess at the corners of his mouth. Beer dripping from a rogue tuft at the chin. A beer cloud floating round his entire head, fractions of an inch above the fro in a dirty nimbus. His blood may've been nothing but beer, for all Steve knew.

"What's up, Steve?" he asked.

Steve just shook his head. Stephanie handed him his beer and he sipped it, joining the guy beside him in a none-too-subtle go at tit gazing.

"Yeah," the guy said. "Just having a good old time."

And then Steve felt a burning stare on his right cheek. Stephanie rimmed up Bones Jones's glass and Steve patiently waited for the motions to resume so he could watch the plump little globes in the clinging red shirt shift and dance. Watching and waiting and yet that damn heat-seeking missile burrowing its way into his face. Stephanie slapped the tap off and picked up the replenished mug, handing it back to the ever-hairy Bones Jones. But still that infernal torch flame cutting along his jaw, around the ear and down the neck. Maybe angry man wanted to peel off his whole face. And then there it was. The shake and dance and then plopping back onto the lucky little stool. Just in time, too, for Steve could endure the searing look no longer.

He whipped his head to the right. Knew he'd catch the fucker grinding his teeth at him. Staring, of course. But he was wrong. Angry man gazed into his beer, maybe hoping to make the contents boil and overflow by sheer hateful force. "Look here, asshole —" had leapt from Steve's mouth, but quickly expired midair to fall into beer rings on the counter, drowning in the pathetic shallows. Steve's brow wrinkled and his nostrils flared, but angry man seemed to totally forget about him. Didn't even bother to notice Steve's rare show of bold-faced defiance. Maybe fighting some nasty inner demon and swearing by the mug in his hands he'd flush it out. He took a big drink and Steve turned away from him.

"Bones! It's your turn to shoot, man." Some guy

Steve had only seen a couple of times in the place before stood halfway between the bar and the pool table. Both his hands were wrapped around a pool stick with its butt on the floor. "Hey . . . Bones."

Bones Jones engrossed in a conversation with the red-faced guy beside Steve. He turned when he heard a woman's voice. The lady who'd tugged on his shirt earlier. Steve didn't think she'd moved once from her seat in the booth since he'd arrived a beer and a half ago.

"What?" Beer dribbled down the side of Bones Jones's glass, over his fingers and onto the carpet at his ragged steel-toed boots. Bare metal showed in parts where heavy things in the past had slammed against his foot.

"It's your turn."

Incomprehension somehow found a spot to rest among the black forest on his face. "Oh," he said, bursting into motion, a second too soon for his sluggish body to respond. The glass slipped from wet fingers and clunked off the gray metal of his boots, bouncing and spinning off the carpet, spilling all the beer out in a diluvial fan. "Aw, shit."

Steve couldn't look anymore. He knew he'd start to laugh if he did. But that didn't stop the guy next to him, of course. An eruption of laughter so forceful his face reddened by two whole orders of magnitude. Steve buried his face in his beer.

"Bones," Stephanie said, shaking her head without a smile. "Pick the mug up, will you?"

"I know, I know." He bent over, laughing along with red-faced guy.

And then a chuckle from the corner of the room. A chuckle into a moderate laugh and finally climaxing into choking spasms. Steve himself almost choked on his beer. He turned to look at angry man, gone all crimson and laughing, one hand pressed against an eye that may've been working itself loose through the vibrations, the other hand slapping his knee. Steve's wide eyes softened and soon he couldn't help but add a few chuckles of his own.

"See," red-faced guy said between laughs. "Told you all you had to do . . ." Teeth bared, stretched lips pushing against a face engorged with blood. "Was drink up."

Then the guy totally lost it. Bones Jones laughed so hard he barely had the strength to put his empty mug back on the counter.

"You going to want another?" Stephanie reached for the mug.

Bones Jones couldn't answer. Just nodded and laughed while the rest of the bar laughed with him. Even Steve. And full on in it now. Laughing so hard himself he dared not take a sip of beer. And once-so-angry man could've been on the verge of bursting his pancreas. But he didn't seem to care. His face squeezed into a grinning ball.

"You guys are children," Stephanie said, pouring yet another beer.

And of course the eruptions expanding the bar's walls. Steve set his beer on the counter so it wouldn't spill. Not that he'd mind much. Didn't even want the beer. For a second, with all the whooping around him, he considered the further merriment to follow an 'accidental' slip of his own mug to the floor.

"Nothing but children."

Stephanie slid the beer across the counter and plopped onto her stool. She grabbed the remote, turned up the volume to drown out the laughter. But, of course, this only made the guys laugh harder.

Bones Jones retrieved his mug. Oblivious to the long hair pasted to the lip of the glass, pointing toward his mouth, maybe trying to join the hirsute Utopia thriving on his chin. He tipped back the mug, drank and laughed again; beer streaming from his mouth. And red-faced guy slapping Bones Jones's pencil-thin arm, sloshing beer down the side of his glass.

Steve shook his head, spasms in death rattles. He turned to look at once-angry man. Eyes open and fixed on Steve. His laughs sputtered to a halt. Brows dipped. Steve couldn't stop himself so quickly. His laughs skidded sideways into the ever-wrinkling face. Angry once again.

"Come on, Bones! You going to take your shot or what?"

Steve didn't see Bones Jones's departure. Only heard it. A swift rustling of clothing and a creaking of bone, then a void filled with the eventual clack of billiard balls. Steve had stopped laughing but refused to turn away. Angry man with acid face wasn't going to intimidate him. Steve wiped his mouth and stared back.

"What the fuck's so funny?" angry man asked. "My friend lost his beer."

"Yeah, I know," Steve said.

"How'd you like it if you lost your beer, huh?"

Steve took a sip from his mug. "I wouldn't."

"And don't forget it." Angry man pointed at him then turned away.

"What?"

Steve looked around him but no one else had heard. The TV blared and Stephanie's eyes and ears were glued to it. Red-faced guy stared at her tits. "Get me another Wild Turkey, would you, Steph?" he asked. Bones Jones and his opponent traded insults and laughs over the soiled expanse of green felt. The girl in the booth tugged at his shirt again, maybe trying to get his attention, to get him to notice that she'd been the one who'd picked the Supertramp song blasting from the jukebox. Then the door opened and a flurry of snow blew in with two big guys in flannel and jeans. Steve didn't know them. Just as he didn't know most of the people there. Not really. He felt alone. And those he did know were isolated in separate rooms or noises or bulging female anatomy. It was just Steve. And angry man of course.

So Steve turned back to unload on him. Give him

a good piece of his mind. But angry man had turned away, leaning across the bar, unscrewing a blue Christmas light from its humble berth on a green plastic cord. The whole line went out. Angry man sat back on his stool and looked about him, finding a stack of napkins, pulling them over to his area

"What the hell's the idea?" Stephanie asked.

Angry man ignored her. He folded the innocent little bulb in a napkin.

Stephanie up and to the bar, directly across from Steve. "Come on, Henry, put the light back."

Steve cradled his beer, glancing down to the end of the bar. Red-faced guy's obnoxious voice droning on and on, shooting the shit with the two fellows who'd come in with the snow. All laughs and clinks of glass. Then falling silent. Greedy gulps of beer and oxygen. Wholly unaware of the Christmas light thievery. And Bones Jones's singing way in the back joined by a female's, probably booth-girl's, together almost overpowering the speakers. So they were oblivious, too. Too far away to notice anything as insignificant as one line of Christmas cheer being snuffed under methodical and mirthless fingers.

"The lady's talking to you, you know," Steve said.

Angry man pushed the little bundle he'd made to the center of the countertop. A quick smile spread then just as quickly faded, watching the object, making sure it wouldn't move. His mug up and drained in a few mighty chugs. A wipe across the mouth. Holding the mug in a steady hand. Eyes squinted a moment before sudden animation brought the glass screaming down onto the little white bundle. A feeble smash swallowed by a heavy whack, silencing the patrons, turning around now, craning necks, leaning on pool sticks and barstools to gawk at angry man in his corner.

Stephanie charged the length of the bar. Finger wags and face steaming. "I think you've had enough." She swiped the empty mug from the countertop. "You're cut off."

Angry man shrugged, scowling as he carefully unfolded the napkin.

"Aw, come one, Steph," red-faced guy said. "It's Christmas. So the guy's a little wound up, let him have another." His mug in beer-spilling scepter sweeps. "On me."

"Oh, no," Steve said. "Guy's definitely had enough." He swallowed hard. Couldn't even imagine choking down more beer he was so agitated. "He's fucking cocked."

Stephanie pointed the mug at angry man. "I think you need to leave."

He grunted and picked blue bits of glass from the rubble on the napkin.

"Yeah, time to go," Steve said.

"Christmas, remember, Steph?" red-faced guy said. "Anybody in this goddamn place remember what that is?"

Once he'd had a nice little handful of blue shards, angry man spun on his stool, glowering at Steve with all the bad-will-towards-man he could muster. He slipped in a sharp blue piece of Christmas glass, chomping it to even smaller fragments then into dust before inserting a brand new piece, keeping his stare fixed on Steve. And he just kept on chomping, kept grinding down glass. Then he opened his mouth. Dull blue angel dust. He popped in another piece to chomp, grind, swallow and glitter. His tongue a strip of beach, littered with sparkling diamonds. Worthless, of course. And soon another piece of glass placed between the teeth.

"What the hell is wrong with you?" Stephanie slammed the empty mug on the counter and matched angry man's corrosive stare with her own. "I told you to get the fuck out. Now! What about that don't you understand?"

Another little blue sliver fished from his palm. He smiled, adding more wrinkles to a face already buckling under pressure from a dense evil from somewhere deep beneath the skin, muscle, brain. And crushing glass to sand.

Steve was hot. About ready to jump off his stool and throttle the guy. But he held his ground, refusing to look away, but not saying a single word. Too hot for speech. It would come out all jumbled and stupid if he'd try to talk now. So he held his beer, his stare and whatever sliver of pride angry man hadn't yet consumed.

"Yeah, man," red-faced guy said. "Maybe you should head on home, cool off, kick your feet up, you know?"

Angry man kept smiling, kept crunching down the demolished bulb, kept shooting acid-filled missiles at Steve.

The two men talking to red-faced guy had shut up. They stepped past their buddy into a cramped silence. One flanked Steve, the other a few steps ahead, three stools from angry man. But angry man didn't pay any attention to these burly men. Just kept smiling and smashing at Steve.

"What are you waiting for, buddy?" one of the burly men asked.

Steve risked a sideways glance. The man who'd spoken, the one further from him, raised his eyebrows, waiting for an answer. Burly man flanking Steve cracked the knuckles of an oversized fist. He smelled of wet dog. His jacket glistened with droplets. More liquid in the form of angry man's blood would go unnoticed, leaching into the thick red fabric.

And then between these two giants slipped Bones Jones, all two hundred and six bones of him, stopping beside his friend, raising his hand and waving it before his eyes. "Hey, Henry. Hey man, snap out of it." He bent down, leaned in; his dirty, overgrown beard braving angry man's hydrochloric gaze. Bubbling and smoking. The vapors from the orbs billowing out and enveloping Bones Jones, the burly men and angry man's adopted enemy. But Steve sat in silence, near-choking with a beer in his hands. And the beer growing warmer as the seconds ticked by.

Crunching hypnotized. "Fucking kill everyone in this bar without a thought." But only Steve and Bones Jones had heard it. At least that's what Steve believed seeing as no one else betrayed the least bit of shock. "Rip them to pieces, goddamn little pieces of meat." Hypnotized and crunching still.

"I know, I know," Bones Jones said. He waved his hand directly in front of angry man's glare. "Hey, hey."

Blue speckles on the lower lip, unnoticed, unfelt. "Fucking meat's all they are, nothing but soft, weak meat and blood."

"Hey, hey, Henry." Bones Jones still waving. "Snap out of it, man, come on." Waving. "Get your head on straight."

Red trickling from the blue. "Blood and blood and blood and meat—"

Bones Jones put a hand on his shoulder and shook. "Henry, hey."

Angry man turned his scowl on Bones Jones, momentarily, before spreading confusion took over.

"You all right? Huh?" Bones Jones shook once more then, noticing the glint of recognition in angry man's eyes, smiled and patted him on the arm. "All right, all right, you're all right, man."

"Get your fucking hand off me," angry man said. And then it all went out of his face, leaving behind a barren wasteland.

"This is the last time I'm telling you," Stephanie said.

"Yeah, yeah," Bones Jones said, waving at Stephanie. "He knows. He's with me." He leaned in once again. "You ready to get out of here, Henry?"

Angry man was dazed. He wiped his lip, looked up at his friend. "I guess."

Red-faced guy jumped from his stool, quite possibly for the first time since he'd sat his ass down, and stood between the burly men.

Bones Jones offered a hand, but angry man waved it away. He stood up, pushed himself from the bar, swaying with eyes almost crossed. "Nothing weak meat but blood and . . ." he said then stopped, focusing his efforts on uncrossing his eyes, staring out at everyone in confusion. Then nothing but hatred. He turned to his only friend in the place.

"Ready when you are," Bones Jones said.

Angry man shrugged then staggered on, approaching the burly men, knuckle-cracking with blank faces. And now a sinister smile plastered to the hatred-for-all-man. But he didn't look at the burly men. Instead he turned to Steve and opened his mouth wide. Blood and sparkles. Steve closed his eyes. When he'd opened them again, when his stomach had stopped kicking other tender organs within, angry man had already passed between two mountains, cackling and coughing his way to the door. Bones Jones followed, thin mountain himself, a slender cut of Matterhorn, passing knuckle cracks and faces full of blood and heat. Out the first set of doors. A jingle of bells, some more cackling, coughing and then shuffles into nothing. For a few moments, no one moved. But then booth girl burst from the pool room, blasting open the door, blinking away a sudden rush of snow.

"Where the hell are you going, Bones?" she asked.

"Got to get him home." Muffled by distance and wind.

"But what about me?"

"Find your own way home."

"Asshole."

Booth girl slammed the door, stormed back to her

seat, arms crossed and pouting. Eventually the other pool player strode over to her and it wasn't long before she was tugging at the tail of his flannel when he leaned over to dump balls into pockets.

Red-faced guy and the burly men laughed, plopped back on their stools, chugged beer and rolled eyes at each others' statements: "Could've pounded that little fucker to pulp," "Made him wet his pants," "What kind of freak eats light bulbs?"

Stephanie wiped down the bar. "That guy gives me the creeps." She stared out through the glass not closed up by shudders, scanning a two-inch strip of falling snow. "Next time he comes in, I'll tell him to get his ass back out."

Steve turned to the bar and set down his mug and elbows.

Red-faced guy slapped Steve on the arm. "What's that guy got against you, anyway?"

"Hell if I know." Steve sipped lukewarm beer.

"He's fucking crazy is all," Stephanie said. She pushed herself atop her stool, grabbed the remote and whipped through TV stations.

"I just wish that guy would've tried to hit me," one burly man said. "Man, I could've popped his head like a zit."

The three laughed at that.

Steve kept choking down his beer, ignoring everything else around him. The blinding Christmas lights and blaring television and chuckling badasses were almost lost in the act of constricting throat muscles. The beer was piss and swallowing had become a glass-sharded pain in the neck.

"All right, all right," red-faced guy said. "Let's leave the poor sucker alone. It's Christmas." He stared into this mug. "Time of good cheer." He smiled weakly and looked at his two friends. They seemed expectant. A hearty laugh of a sudden and he raised his mug. "Let's get another beer!"

"Yeah!"

"All right!"

Up and down and soon the three stared into empty glass depths. Burps and laughter. Stephanie filling their mugs and they filling their eyes with her tits. Red-faced guy asked for another shot of whiskey. She turned around and before long three sets of eyes crammed themselves with her full, soft bottom. But she paid little attention to the crudities at the bar. More important things were happening on the tube.

Steve was disgusted with the burly mob and their brazen faces. Disgusted with the bartender parading a figure built of curvaceous lust that he'd never get to touch. Disgusted with booth girl tugging on the belt loops of the guy standing over her, rubbing his pool stick and giggling. Disgusted with the sights, the smells, the sounds. Steve was disgusted with it all. He'd been here too long, become to familiar. He'd sullied himself with the rest of these wastrels and now he just wanted to go home and be alone. Maybe clean up a bit. Erase the stains and odors clinging to clothes and skin. He looked at his beer. Disgusted with that, too. He choked down the rest of it and felt a little sick. Cleared his throat a couple of times but the slimy disgust wouldn't go down. Caught in the soft, pink flesh. Disgust along with the shimmering memory of blue glass shards.

"Well," he said, standing up. "I think it's time I went home."

"What?" Red-faced guy swung around in his chair.

"Yeah, it's getting late." Steve threw his only dollar on the counter.

"It's still the afternoon," red-faced guy said.

"Sorry, that's all I got, Steph." Steve patted the bar and pulled on his jacket.

"Don't worry about it," she said.

"You can't go," red-faced guy said.

Steve zipped up. "Well, I am." He turned to leave.

"At least have a shot with us before you go."

A giggle to the side. Steve turned to the poolroom, saw the guy with the pool stick reach under booth girl's shirt, smiling. Christmas lights winked against the far wall. The guy turned, throwing Steve a knowing glance, but Steve was looking through him, even through the flashing lights, merely watching their shadows move in sequence along paneling.

"Ah . . . no," Steve said. He shrugged. "I've already had more than enough."

"Come on, now, man." Red-faced man looked to his friends who had their shots of Wild Turkey firmly in hand. He nodded at Steve. "One shot's not going to hurt you. It's for the holidays."

"Nope." Steve shook his head. "Have to go."

"All right, suit yourself." Red-faced guy held his shot in the air and the burly men followed. "Here's to guys that don't drink too much so that guys like us can drink even more."

"Yeah!"

"Let's get cocked!"

"Merry Christmas!"

And they all downed their whiskey in great manly throwbacks while Stephanie shook her head, returning her concentration to the lofty TV screen, turning up the volume another notch. Booth girl giggled and Steve heard her guy say, "Come on, baby" just before he opened the door. The jingle of bells overhead, "Merry Christmas!" once again from a red-face and finally, gratefully, the metal creak and wooden slap of the door. Steve pushed through the second door and was greeted by a quick shower of snow. He had to hold his head down and to the side to keep snow from piling up on his face, in his eyes. Really coming down now and the parking lot absolutely covered in a chaste cotton blanket.

A massive plow screeched by with its yellow caution lights swirling and then disappearing. Steve patted his jacket pocket and ground to a halt a few feet from his truck. Nothing in it. He searched through his jacket, through his pants, turned around and slowly walked back to the door, following his footprints for a glimmer from his keys. He almost stooped at one point, but soon realized that the metallic sheen was nothing more than the foil wrapper from a bag of chips. His keys weren't anywhere to be seen. Through his pockets one more time and then stopping abruptly. Fear on the face. He marched toward the truck, peered through the driver's window. There they hung, his keys and keychain, unattainable, from the ignition.

"Goddamnit."

He pulled out his wallet. Flips through plastic. Maybe a spare key in some forgotten slot or fold. But there was nothing. And then he remembered he'd taken it out and put in on his keychain because the old one had worn out. The old key lay amongst a litter of mostly useless objects in the junk drawer of the kitchen of his house. Had been for quite a while.

"Goddamnit, goddamnit."

He knew the doors would be locked but he checked them anyway. Then peering through the passenger window until it fogged up. He wiped it clean, took one last glance at his keys and finally backed away. All around him he searched. For who knows what. Snow kept piling on. Steve pulled on his gloves and looked over at the bar. No way in hell he was heading back inside to bum a ride. He didn't know anyone, anyway, except maybe red-faced guy. But he didn't even know his name. Besides, the guy was busy drinking himself silly. Probably be at it all day and night into the next day. Probably be sauced until Old Saint Nick himself showed up, maybe hoping to share a nip with him.

"To hell with that."

Steve walked to the edge of the road. A couple of cars passed. He scanned both ways. More cars approaching, others fleeing into the arms of a blinding storm. But it wasn't really all that bad out. Could make it home in half an hour, forty-five minutes tops. He clapped his hands, pulled the hood to his sweatshirt from beneath his jacket and over his baseball-capped head. The wind would be blowing against him most of the way home. It was going to be cold.

"Goddamn my luck."

Steve clapped his hands one more time then started down the road to his warm home with the warm couch and comforting warm glow of his TV.

A ring of the doorbell followed by a series of short knocks. Steve got up from his couch and went to answer the door. He parted the blinds, peeked through. His son's smiling face greeted him. A bright red and white winter's cap formed to his skull; the earflaps pulled down and tied beneath the chin. He waved and said something too muffled for Steve to make out. A little red ball jiggled atop the knit hat. Steve opened the door.

"Hey, Dad. Merry Christmas."

"Where the hell did you get that ridiculous hat?"

Kevin sighed. "I said Merry Christmas, Dad."

"Yeah, Merry Christmas." Steve noticed a present in his son's left hand. He looked back at a nervous smile. "You steal that thing from Linus or something?"

The little red ball danced when Kevin shook his head. "It's from Aunt Cheryl. She gave me it last year for Christmas, so I thought it'd be appropriate to wear it tonight."

"You going to see Aunt Cheryl?"

"Well, yeah, I always see her on Christmas."

Steve spotted a car alongside the road. The parking lights on but the headlights cold and dead. In the dark, Steve could barely make out the driver taking random glances at the house. Hardly more than a kid. And black.

"Nice car," Steve said. "I take it it's not yours."

"No."

The kid sneaked another glance. He caught Steve's and instantly looked away to the road or maybe the rearview.

"A little young for you to be hanging around with, isn't he?" Steve asked.

"Come on, Dad, quit busting my balls."

Steve shrugged.

Kevin held out his present. "Well, here you go. It's not much, but it's something."

Steve took the present, raised it to his ears and shook. He waved the gift and said, "Come on in, then, you're letting the heat out."

Kevin turned and signaled to the driver to hold on a minute. He entered the house, closing the storm door behind him.

"Your present didn't come in yet," Steve said. "Didn't order it until a couple days ago."

Kevin put his hands behind his back. "That's OK." Looking down and pawing at the doormat with a leather boot.

"No, I'm just kidding." Steve went into the living room. "Why don't you take off your coat and hat—you know, stay awhile?"

"Can't." Kevin pulled off his gloves. "Aunt Cheryl's expecting us. We're already a little late."

"Take your hat off at least." Steve came back into the kitchen with a large present in his hands. "You look like a goofball."

Kevin rolled his eyes and untied the earflaps, removing the hat and hanging it over the end of a chair.

110

Steve placed the present in his son's hands.

"Boy, it's lighter than it looks." Kevin peered around its sides, underneath and through slightly open folds in the paper.

"Well, are you going to keep gawking at it or you going to open it?"

Kevin set the present on the table. He noticed a small Christmas tree on a stand in the corner. "Boy, you went all out on decorations this year." One pathetic strand of lights barely circled the dwarfed evergreen. The only ones in the house.

"Yeah." Steve glanced at the tree. "Figured I'd do it up big this time."

His son began unwrapping his present. It was in a big generic cardboard box. No labels or warnings or even arrows to point out which part of the box was up. Packing tape sealed the top tight enough to deflect a tactical nuclear strike.

"Think I'm going to need a knife for this," Kevin said.

Steve flipped over the box. "It doesn't matter which end you open. I wouldn't think you'd be picky about a thing like that."

"Jesus Christ, Dad."

"All right, I'm sorry." Steve tapped the box. "Just open it."

His son looked at him with disgust. A face familiar to Steve.

"OK, I said I'm sorry." Steve shrugged. "Look, do you want the gift or not?"

Kevin considered his dad for a moment then tore into the box, pulling out scores of newspaper balls, scattering them all over the table and floor. Eventually, he got to the present's nougat and yanked it out among another eruption of newspaper. In his hands and staring at it, confused.

"A soccer ball?"

"Yeah." Steve coughed. "I remember how much you loved to kick it around when you were a kid and thought that you probably didn't have one anymore, so there you go."

"Wow." Kevin squeezed the ball then bounced it against his knee a couple of times "A soccer ball. Don't know what to say."

"There's a coupon, too," Steve said, pointing. "Turn it around."

Kevin flipped over the ball to see a big coupon hastily cut and taped to the smooth surface.

"It's for a free large pizza," Steve said.

"Yeah, I see that."

"I know you like pizza."

"Yeah, thanks." Kevin spun the ball and tossed it in the air. "Thanks a lot."

He rolled the ball in his hands. An uncomfortable silence. Just the sound of skin on leather. Steve felt the need to add something, maybe about how good Pizza Heaven's pizza was or how fun it was to kick the living snot out of a soccer ball, but he picked up the present from the table instead.

"What's in here?"

"I don't know, you'll have to open it."

Steve peeled back the wrapping paper. A deluxe beard trimmer sat in the palm of his hand. "I never wear a beard."

"Yeah, I know," Kevin said, still rolling the ball. "But in case you do, I figured it would come in handy."

"But I hate beards." Steve gazed at the trimmer. "Any facial hair at all drives me up a wall."

"Yeah, well, you're getting up there." Tossing the ball in the air again. "And I know how you old timers like to grow your beards out all bushy and stuff."

"What, like Santa Claus?"

Kevin caught the ball and looked at his dad. "No . . . well, I don't know." Bouncing the ball against his knee.

"Look like Santa Claus if you want or Jeremiah fucking Johnson or don't use it at all, whatever, it's yours. Do whatever you want." The ball went flying, over the table and landing at the bottom of the stairwell. "It's supposed to be a gift."

Steve went after the ball. "No, no, I like it." He picked it up and threw it back to his son. "I'll find a use for it." He held out the trimmer and made sheep-sheering motions in the air. "Maybe I can use it on my legs."

Kevin chuckled. "Or your back."

Steve smiled. He dropped the trimmer on the kitchen table.

Another moment of silence. Both of them gazed around the room, maybe hoping for an object to pop out, grab their attention, maybe turn into a topic of conversation for a few minutes. Kevin saw a Christmas card, the only one in sight, folded out and resting on a little shelf against the wall. He pointed with a feeble finger. Maybe going to ask about its origins. But his dad beat him to the punch.

"Your mom called for you, you know."

Kevin's mouth hung open, still wrapped around the lonely Christmas card. But then it closed because he couldn't think of anything to say. He looked at the ground, squeezing the soccer ball over and over again.

"Quite a while back." Steve kicked at a leg to the kitchen table. "Wants to know if you're all right." He looked up. "Maybe you should call her."

Kevin kept his gaze on the floor. "Yeah, maybe I will, at Aunt Cheryl's or something."

"You shouldn't give her a reason to worry about you, you know," Steve said. "She can get wild notions in her head she can't shake free. You know how screwy she can get."

"Yeah." Kevin now watching the Christmas lights change on the miserable, little tree. "Especially with that asshole boyfriend she's got living with her."

Steve didn't say anything. Couldn't say anything. He knew he was treading on ground far too alien for him to be bothering with. Best thing to just ride it out, maybe give a word of encouragement, a pat on the back. A slice of pizza at the very least, if he'd had one.

"Yeah . . ." Steve's son sweeping the room with restless eyes. "So, looks like I got to get going soon. My ride's waiting."

"Yeah, yeah, sure." Steve nodded, rubbed his chin. "Thanks for the trimmer."

"Hey, thanks for the soccer ball." Kevin held it up. He found his gloves, pulled them on, then made for the door.

"Don't forget your stupid ass hat." Steve tossed it to him.

"Oh, yeah." He put it on and nodded and the ball on top bobbed around.

"God, you look fucking ridiculous," Steve said.

Kevin held out an arm. The other cradled the ball to his side. "I'm walking out of here with a soccer ball. Can't get anymore ridiculous than that."

Steve wore a little wry grin.

"Don't say it," his son said. "Don't even open your mouth." He opened the door and looked back. "Merry Christmas, Pop."

Still with the stupid grin.

Kevin shook his head. "I swear sometimes you should be the son."

"Hey," and grinning. "I didn't say anything."

"Thankfully."

"I mean, not one crack about K-Y or anal beads or anything." Steve stopped to consider that, then burst into laughter. "I said crack."

"I'm out of here." Kevin out the storm door, trudging through the snow, up the small incline to where the car and its driver sat.

Steve had the door open. He yelled to his son

before he could drop into the car. "Where you staying at?"

Kevin threw the ball inside the car. "Aunt Cheryl's."

"I know that, I mean later." His breath misted, floating from the porchlight's glare. "You know, where you living at?"

"Here and there. Don't worry about it."

His son got in the car and shut the door. He waved then looked away before Steve could wave back, but Steve only stood still, holding open the door with an elbow, shivering slightly from the chill. The car drove off and gave a couple short blasts from the horn. Steve watched it dissolve into the shadowy depths of the road, cutting through the impossible black of even greater depths of endless forest. His breath mist followed after.

The door closed. Porch light off. Just Steve and the beard trimmer and the pathetic little Christmas tree.

GUNS AND FAGGOTS

"What the hell's the deal with the t-shirt?" Ted asked.

Ozzie swallowed the bit of sandwich he'd been chewing. "It's a Christmas gift."

"Yeah, but what's with it? You don't hunt."

The sandwich hung from Ozzie's fingers. He looked down at his shirt. In bold letters:

My Wife Yes,
My Dog Maybe . . .

Then a revolver facing point blank and:

My Gun NEVER!!

"Doesn't say anything about hunting," he said.

Ted shook his head. "Doesn't have to."

"Doesn't have to," Ozzie said. "Why don't you try making some sense."

Ted took a drink of his Coke.

Steve cut in. "I think what Ted's trying to say is that why would you be so adamant about having your gun taken away when you don't even use it for hunting."

Ted nodded.

"I hunt," Ozzie said.

Ted almost choked on his Coke. "What, when you were twelve?"

"No, until about eighteen, but I used to hunt a lot as a kid." Ozzie turned red and kept chewing. "Still got the same rifle."

"Yeah," Steve said. "But you don't hunt anymore, haven't in a while, so that's why Ted's asking you about your shirt."

"It's for protection."

Ted let out a big laugh and Steve and Dave soon joined him. Donnie didn't seem to be paying attention. He spooned yogurt into his mouth, reading a magazine he'd brought into the break room.

"Man, no way," Ted said. "I've been over your house before, I've seen your rifle. That pathetic piece of shit's collecting dust on a shelf in your basement. Thing's not even loaded."

"How would you know that?" Ozzie completely red.

"I looked."

"You always snoop around people's property?"

"Jesus Christ," Ted said. "It was a fucking gun just lying around so I looked at it." His Coke poised for another swallow. "Besides, I wouldn't trust you with a paintball gun. I had to check."

"Fuck you man, it still works." Ozzie stumbled over some words and coughed. "Put a goddamn hole through anyone that tried to get through my door, that's for sure."

"Whatever," Ted said then drained his Coke.

Ozzie was red, saw red, choked down his sandwich and forced the rest of it into his mouth. He chewed ferociously, heroically. Could've been chewing his tongue.

"Who'd give a shirt like that for Christmas, anyway?" Steve asked. "I mean, I know it wasn't your wife."

Dave grunted and looked at Ozzie, waiting for an answer.

"What's with the third degree?" Still chewing. He had a lot of tongue.

"I'm just curious," Steve said.

Ozzie cleared his throat, drank some soda and cleared his throat again. "Got it from my brother in law."

"Your brother in law?"

"Yeah." Ozzie looked at Steve in confusion. Then he turned to Ted and Dave who both started chuckling. "We thought it was funny, what's wrong with that?"

Dave grunting and laughing. Ted shaking his head. Donnie spooning in the yogurt, flipping pages.

"Nothing, forget it," Steve said.

Ozzie held his arms out and shrugged. "What the fuck?"

"Don't worry about it, Ozzie," Steve said.

"Just pulling your chain," Ted said.

And Dave laughing.

But then everything petered out. No one spoke.

Ozzie rummaged through his brown paper bag to see if there was anything else in there he could grind to pulp. Nothing. He balled up the paper bag and aimed for the garbage can. He hesitated. Maybe considering noshing on the paper wad to vent his anger. He tossed the bag into the can.

"Did your wife think it was funny?" Donnie had set down the magazine to look at Ozzie. One hand held the yogurt container while the other had the plastic spoon.

Steve and Ted and Dave all laughing.

"What?" Ozzie's face still red, still pinched in violence. "Just eat your yogurt and shut the fuck up, Donnie."

"Hey." Donnie with the yogurt and spoon out. "Just asking a question."

"Yeah, well them assholes already asked me a bunch of stupid questions and I don't need a yogurt-eating faggot like you acting like an asshole, too."

"Faggot?" Donnie put the spoon back into the container and set it on the table.

"Yeah, only fags eat yogurt," Ozzie said. "What're you, watching your weight or something, pussy boy?"

The rest of the guys kept silent. Ozzie had finally got himself all pissy and there wasn't any point in adding more fuel to the fire. Except for Dave's occasional grunts. But they went largely unnoticed, anyway.

"Sounds like a whole lot of homophobic hot air." Donnie crossed his arms.

"That's right," Ozzie said. "I'm a homophobe, so what? Better than being a fucking homo."

"I'm no homo."

"Yeah, you are." Ozzie pointed his finger. "You stick up for the blacks, you got nothing good to say about anybody that doesn't dress like they just stepped off a college campus and you don't drink Coke."

"I'm a fag because I don't drink Coke?"

"That's right." Now Ozzie crossed his arms.

"Smug cocksucker. And because you eat yogurt."

"Man," Donnie said, uncrossing his arms. "You've got issues."

"Faggot." And then Ozzie swatted the empty container of yogurt onto the floor.

"What the hell, man?" Donnie shook his head.

Ted noticed how absolutely red Ozzie had become. "Hey, come on now, guys. Knock it off."

Dave stared at Ozzie and didn't move a damn muscle.

"What're you looking at?" Ozzie waved his hand at Dave. "Mind your own goddamn business."

Dave grunted then smiled.

"Calm down now, Ozzie," Ted said. "Calm down."

"I'll calm down when I'm good and ready." Ozzie glared at Donnie. "And what the fuck are you grinning at?"

"Nothing," Donnie said. "Absolutely nothing."

"Fuck you, faggot." Donnie pushed the table.

Donnie smirked.

Dave grinned and grunted, staring at Ozzie.

"What're you a fag, too?" Ozzie stood up.

"Calm the hell down, will you?" Ted motioned Ozzie to sit.

Ozzie just shook his head. "Fuck you, assholes." He headed for the door. "I don't need to be sitting at a table full of faggots."

"Ozzie—"

And then he opened the door to storm out onto the work floor. In its recovery from the violent pull it sailed back toward the frame then suddenly slowed just before settling into its berth with a graceful little click. A moment of silence as the guys looked at each other. All except for Steve. He stared down at the table, watching the spray from the light above shake on the gently rocking surface.

"Punk," Dave said.

And this time everybody turned to look at Dave. "Give the guy a break, he's having troubles with his wife," Steve had said. But then Dave just grunted again, leaving Ted and Donnie to shake their heads and talk about Ozzie until they got sick of that and changed the subject to something less acidic. Only a few minutes left in the lunch break. The two had decided to spend it in a harmless debate on the values of a 3-4 versus a nickel defense. And football wasn't even their favorite sport.

Steve didn't have the heart for the conversation. He'd usually offer some tidbit when it came to sports. Especially football, his favorite one to watch after baseball. But it wasn't in him now. Maybe more akin to the scattered light wavering on the fake woodgrain of the table. Just kind of there, vibrating, and yet unheard, unseen by everyone else. So with Steve. At least that's what his face projected, if someone had been watching. Just to pass the last remaining moments of his break in anonymity. To forget about minor explosions and yogurt and red-faced nonsense. To pretend for a while that guns and faggots didn't exist.

The last hour of the shift on the very same workday Mac shambled up to where Steve sat at the console with the plastic guard lifted, operating the press from the screen. Steve had seen him from the corner of his eye. He just knew the big, greasy lump of a man was going to drop his leaden ass at the console's side.

"Having troubles?" Mac asked.

"Gate's sticking." Steve touched the screen. "It's plugged up is all."

"Oh."

Steve brought down the guard, flipped the switch

into Auto and leaned back in the chair, watching the transfer complete itself on the monitors atop the console. Mac rested an arm against one of the monitors. He pointed through the entrance leading into the other half of the shop.

"Not much of a press compared to that baby over there, huh?" he said.

Steve looked over at the makeshift, skeletal frame of a press not much taller than six feet and barely wider than the console to his own machine giant. Hoses and wires ran from the top and bottom and sides. Leaching water and nitrogen from the monster press; trying in vain to show its importance even when under the shadow of its much bigger and impressive older brother. For now it sat dormant and cold. Lifeless and empty.

"You mean the Superpress," Steve said.

Mac chuckled. "Going to save the company, huh? Pull us right out of the old shitter?"

Steve turned back to his press. "Don't think it's going to pull much of anything out except for charred ceramic."

"Stuart thinks it'll work," Mac said.

"Yeah?" Watching the screens. "Well Stuart still believes our parts have the best quality on the market."

"You read a copy of the article that went around the shop on Monday?"

"Of course." Steve stood up as the die in the monitor sunk from view. "Everybody read the article. Where'd you think I found out just how shitty our parts are? But it's nothing that we hadn't known all along."

Mac nodded.

"Just a matter of time before the Japanese whomp the piss out of us," Steve said.

"Soon we'll be eating sushi and driving rice burners." Mac let out a green, smeary grin.

Steve picked up his mask, jotted down some numbers on his log sheet while the press cycled anew.

"Fucking ex-wife's got a Honda."

Mac made a choking sound followed by a low rumble of phlegm. He swallowed a couple of times, cleared his throat again then offered Steve another flash of grimy teeth.

"What the hell was that?"

Mac shrugged. "A pack of cigarettes or so."

Steve was about to put on his mask when Mac tapped his arm.

"Hey," he said. "Have you seen the inside of that thing?"

Steve glanced at the Superpress then back at Mac. He shrugged.

"Come on." Mac pushed himself free from the console's gravity. "You got to see this."

Steve set down his mask. Willing to break his routine. He'd answer the whine of the press when he got back. The webs would just take a little longer cooling down, was all.

Mac turned around, halfway to the Superpress, and waved.

"I'm coming," Steve said and followed Mac along three-quarter inch hose running atop the concrete floor to the press.

Mac pulled over an orange chair from the side and slid it against the press. He placed his hand on the frame to steady himself. Going to be a lot of motion for a boulder. He heaved himself up onto the chair with a creak.

"Careful," Steve said. "I don't think that thing's rated for three-hundred pounds."

"You ain't so light yourself, you pot-bellied fuck." Both of Mac's hands clasped the rim of the press. He balanced himself then nodded at Steve. "Get yourself a chair."

Steve pulled one over and soon peeked into the dark column of the press. Graphite dust coated the entire inside. Bits of ceramic and insulation littered the bottom.

Steve picked up his hand and noted the line of soot across his fingers.

"Jesus, the thing's a mess," he said.

"I'm surprised you never looked before." Mac scratched his prickly chin, leaving a smudge under the lip.

"I don't know, the whole thing just seemed like a waste of time."

"It is."

Steve looked over the side, down the machine's back. Electrical wires snaked along diamond-plate into a large green box. Steve jumped off the chair and walked over to it. A big green lid rested on its side behind the box. A red metal label screwed to the top: Hunterdon Transformer Co.

"Where the hell did they dig up this thing from?" Steve asked.

Mac was still gazing into the dirty depths of the Superpress. He looked past it now to the transformer.

"I don't know," he said. "Definitely not around here. Must be from one of the other shops."

"I bet the Japanese don't have one of these babies."

"Our secret weapon." And Mac's green teeth saw light again.

Steve glanced into the transformer's guts then snagged the chair he'd been using and put it back where it belonged. And all the while Mac struggling to get down, never letting a hand slip from his hold on the press. A lot of grunting, a lot of groaning, a whole lot of wheezing. When his feet finally touched down on solid concrete, Mac let out a sigh. Then the usual choking and phlegm roller coaster. Both of his elbows rested against the filthy metal frame. Gasps and wheezes squeezed between the pudgy folds of his arms.

"I'll put this back for you," and Steve removed the chair.

Mac just waved an arm above his head, still

leaning on the cold bars of the Superpress.

"You going to be all right?" Steve asked.

Mac pushed himself off. Face red with a black spot smeared on the forehead. He waved twice and tried to speak. Wheezing and gasping then finally smiling again.

"Yeah, sure," he said. "Never felt better." He coughed, a hand to his chest. "Got to stop overworking myself." Coughing. "Don't pay me enough for all this shit."

Steve cracked his knuckles. Ready to turn and leave.

"Think it's about time I thought about calling it quits," Mac said.

Steve's eyebrows rose. "Really?"

"Yeah, this company's going nowhere and I got enough in my 401K to survive on. I don't need this place."

"Never though I'd hear you say that," Steve said. "Thought we'd be carrying your fat ass out of here after you keeled over the Maintenance workbench."

"Nah, fuck it." He winked. "You and the Japs can keep this place."

Another smile from Mac, but it seemed tired. Only half of his lip moved. Then he turned with a wheeze and a cough and lumbered down the shop, around the corner and out of sight. Out of sight but not out of sound. Coughs still and mucous in the throat. But then these ceased and the echo of nothing rang out from the vaulted ceilings. All sound, all vibrations choked in the clutter of air ducts and water lines.

A hum maybe and Steve remembered that his press still needed unloading. His back then to the big green transformer with the Superpress beside it and returning to his proper workstation. Back to the whine and the grime and the heat of his job.

The sky and roads were clear while Steve buzzed home in his blood-red truck. Snow crusted the grass and trees and eaves of buildings he blew by. Dirty crusty snow along the sides of the road, stuck to the curbs and forming a shield against all the shit and mud and slush the overgrown trucks of the past had whipped out in unclean fans. Dirtied and crusted and protecting until some future overcast day of winter decided to drop down replacements in paratrooping flakes, packing together, crushing together and forming a new pure, white-crusted shell.

But the roads were now clear so Steve wasn't spraying out any dirty fans and neither was the truck in front of him. And the sky looked to be clear for a good long time, allowing the sleeting reserves that waited to be fashioned from ice motes high up in the atmosphere to go on drifting and collecting and watching the big steel beasts zoom beneath on asphalt paths between their distant, packed and crusted cousins.

A little glowing cigarette butt flew out the window of the truck ahead of Steve, followed by a blinking red taillight. The truck took a right without slowing and swerved a bit as the driver corrected its curve back over the yellow lines into the appropriate lane. The cigarette whisked away in Steve's mighty crosswind. He lost sight of it. The cherry glow had already been extinguished. Cold and blind and forever fagged, it smacked against the curb's hard crusted walls and flipped into the snowy wasteland beyond. Steve hadn't seen this either, but he imagined it to be the truth, scanning the rearview for a sign of the stranded cigarette filter. And all the time to the right and disappearing sailed the truck that had jettisoned the useless corpse.

Steve rounded a corner and began the slow ascent leading to the plateau where his house sat neglected and fat and desperately wanting for its lights to be flicked on, its heat to be kicked up, its sore and creaking floorboards to feel the warm, sure tread of its master's feet. But the master wasn't home yet. Only beginning the ascent. And the house could sense the slight tremor in the earth, growing in its bowels. Could feel the windows shake, the shudders quake, the roof tiles murmur against each overlapped brother, louder and louder and about to burst and rain in fragments until Steve's truck would tuck itself safely into the backyard's little niche.

And Steve still ascending. Past neighbors' houses — familiar, cozy, nesting in beds of snow not far from the road. Mailboxes bearing numbers that ascended as well. Numbers for hardworking people just like Steve. Painted or decaled or molded in plastic. Numbers to ensure that these honest individuals would receive their daily mail and delivery pizzas. Numbers in different shapes and colors; some faded, some bright and new. But all nonetheless present to lend the town's citizens, the ascending road's denizens a definite location, a definite importance, a special individual responsibility. Numbers for men and women. Fathers, mothers, husbands, wives pointing and smiling and posing for pictures in the snow for next year's Christmas cards, shipped out and slipped into far-flung mailboxes with different sets of numbers. Numbers to set one house from the other house and the other house, on up through the ranks, ascending, pushing on, pushing forward toward one great big house off the road. And then to stop and settle and let the numbers climb on past into infinity.

But infinity was far away and Steve was only ascending, after all. Only to a point. But it felt good to know that every plot of property from here to his house and even a little beyond was wrapped in the fuzzy, itchless blanket of familiar numbers and faces and pointing fingers and "How you doing, neighbor?"

Familiar things, once again. On his way home from work. Watching the houses and the people and the cars stream by. Allowing the sights to sink in and numb his brain straight down to his steel-covered toes. Feeling the gentle wash and tingles of the familiar world pool in his boots. Letting the smeary images slide off the glass, fall and reassemble themselves on snow-shrouded lawns and ever-stretching lengths of tar out past the hard, frigid ass of his truck. Or maybe he just had the temp cranked too high. Steve backed off the heat. He settled himself once again into his plush cradle, skull snug against the headrest, and watched the smears fall over and over into reassembly.

And the Paki out again. Another familiar feature if not quite in a familiar pose. His hands wrapped around a shovel's handle with the blade sunk into a drift of snow at the driveway's base. Steve added liberal pumps to the brake pedal. Didn't want to blow past the guy and miss what he was up to. A report had to be given to his fellow press operator at work. The guy on third shift. Steve didn't miss a thing. The Paki just stood there; a blank, dark, staring statue. He didn't move even when a gust suddenly flared up from the ground and threw out his flannel, exposing a huge gold medallion banging against his chest. Steve kept pumping and almost stopped, creeping up to the guy. The wind had died and the flannel fell back at his sides. And he just kept staring at the snow in his driveway, smoothed out and pulled all the way to the bottom, around a cinder block with an orange flag on a pole poking up from it. And the snow around the shovel had pushed on past it to flood the man's feet. And a little ways past the feet, the snow trickled into clumps then a dusting that expired just shy of the berm's white line. And Steve inching by, risking long stares, glancing in the rearview for cars that weren't coming. The Paki finally turned his head, rolling dark eyes over sunlight, collecting the heat and light and rolling on still to stab themselves into Steve's naked whites. And Steve could only turn away and blink and give it the gas until his truck was far from creeping and inching. But in the rearview the black eyes yet stabbed. Thankfully, a car climbed after Steve, granting the purpose to use the speed Dodge gave him to cover the embarrassment of his flight. No need to creep and inch. He ascended. And a willing partner flogged him on from behind.

So he climbed past the numbers on the boxes to the houses with the people pointing at trees, a Paki with a spade, lawns full of snow. Then a final curve with a big truck's wide-sweeping grace. Now only a few hundred feet to the plateau where sprawled the Volunteer Fire Department and its lot crammed with cars. Just three houses beyond that and Steve would be home. But he always parked in the back. Especially in winter, since a friend from the VFD plowed his driveway. And the front lawn's incline was too much of a bitch to get out of. So he took a right into the VFD, zipping past a truck unloading beer and the cars lining the parking lot all the way down to a dirt road on the left. He slowed the blood-red beast and clawed his way through potholes toward his yard.

Bad Adolph barked his head off. You could only see his painted name from this vantage. And he came pounding turf from his doghouse and choked on the chain, falling short of the climb to the dirt road. Steve waved and laughed and kept driving. And then his driveway. He coasted into the bare patch of earth. His truck shut down, sighed and drifted into sleep. Tired of climbing hills, tired from hauling Steve's chubby butt halfway across the county.

Steve was tired, too. A pause a few moments in the cab, staring at his yard. Snow stretched back to his house. A few trees, a burning barrel, footprints leading to the back porch the only breaks in the clean white sheet. But then he noticed another set of prints running down the hill, just inside his neighbor's property, disappearing at the dirt road. Probably from one of the kids up the hill, in one of those rundown buildings across the street. Steve didn't have kids living with him anymore. Nor his flanking neighbors. Steve knew it had to have been one of them little fuckers. In the summer there'd be tipped over tricycles and Wiffle bats. But for now, trespassing footprints.

It started to cool in the once-cozy cab. He opened the door and plopped himself down on familiar ground. The grates and slides of his driveway gave way to the crunch of snow. The neighbor's backdoor swung open and slapped into place. The neighbor through the crunch in oversized snow boots. A brown trash bin in his hands. Still wearing the rainbow-striped robe with the nylon cord.

"Hey, Steve."

"Hey."

And they passed. One to burn, one to bury himself in the TV's glare. Steve could hear the garbage dump down the barrel's rusted throat. Right next to the piece of shit Camaro. Stuck in snow. And other things behind Steve. A dirt road chockfull of potholes, Bad Adolph barking, streets that went up and down and the numbers that followed, a Paki boring dark eyes into the brash skulls of staring fools, cars zipping rights and lefts out of the mainstream, the orange burn of cigarettes and the dirt-crusted curbs that tried to make some order, some sense of it all.

But it all made sense to Steve. Always had, always would. Or so he believed. Without even giving it so much as a passing thought. Passing thoughts, yes, passing thoughts. But they weren't in his head. On the outside. Things to be seen. Items to sink into gray plumpness before being ejected in wet, smelly clumps. And yet they were all behind him. In the past, in the distance, lying and sticking on cold pavement.

But what if a blizzard came through and draped all these familiar objects, people, places under the thick crush of snow? Where would the everyday signposts be to point his way home? Where his home?

Passing thoughts, still passing thoughts that seldom found their way into Steve's head. More the TV. Consumed by what was on and what might be on later. And that was all. And food of course. But that was a given. A foregone conclusion. A familiar thing.

It was the last cold, wet struggle of winter. Somewhere around when Caesar got the knife in his back. And always around this time, Steve had to get his truck's registration and inspection renewed. But there were more pressing concerns. The Big Wheels had ordered a meeting for the end of the week. All the plants were expected to attend. This sudden cattle-call had prompted the middlemen to summon their own meeting to help break the fall or else present a show of good faith and dispel any doubts whatsoever as to the bloodlessness of their hands. They hadn't caused the fall and everybody knew it. But they decided to put the show on regardless and wear the sad, tired costumes they always wore when handing the shop bad news. And this was going to be bad news, or so the rumors went.

Steve quickly scanned the people filed against the walls, from the sink all the way around the room to the door. The space between the sink and the door was reserved for the middlemen and they could easily be distinguished from everyone else by their ties, ironed shirts, clean faces and, of course, the sad, tired costumes. They'd been dusted off before entering the cafeteria, but Steve could almost smell the stink of disuse and stagnation. Someone in a corner sneezed when the plant manager brushed something from a navy blue lapel.

And flanking the middlemen were the engineers. Really in a class all their own, although they looked similar to the middlemen minus the ties and sad, tired costumes. They'd no game to play so they hadn't the need for special attire. Always have their jobs if they wanted them. If not here, than at some other shop, some other company. Their particular skills in all the dealings of employed humans were necessary, sought out, brought on board by the powers that be. From process techs to systems analysts all the way up to those who design ingenious ways to kill and quiet people for the State.

Then the door cracked open, a dark face appearing around its edge. David King, the black engineer, entered the room, nodding, parking himself beside the men beside the middlemen. The room's clusters of hushed discussions died for a moment as faces swept toward the front then back to their partners on the sides. The mumbles began anew. David paid no mind, only looked over the heads of the outlying workers with eyes of a hardness unlike anyone else's in the room. Stoic and standing with arms behind his back.

And Steve, too, turned away from David's severe gaze to watch a small yellow tag on a string hanging from the screen to a heating duct, swaying in the breeze, slapping against metal. Constant, ever constant and Steve took comfort in knowing that something moved in the room that hadn't been summoned, there just to be there, swinging in the wind, marking the passing of time, marking the force necessary to heat the roomful of men and women in ties, steel-toed boots or neither. It was there and didn't care but did its job just the same. Maybe a yellow flag flapped in David King's head. Who knew? Not Steve. For Steve was there to be there but he had to care because maybe his job was on the line.

A few more people crammed themselves into the room. The chairs at the tables in the center had long since been filled. Every tiny niche along the walls bulged with bellies and shoulders and legs and feet. And, of course, the front reserved for the soon-to-be-speaking managers in their costumes with the engineers at attention, watching the human flesh bubble on the walls' skin. Except for David. Hadn't yet removed his gaze from somewhere slightly above the refrigerator at the back of the room. So these recent employees worked their way between the tribes of the walls and the tribes of the tables to stand somewhere in the middle of the congestion. Individual dots taking up the slots. Once-free electrons, broken long ago from the human nucleus, setting up static residence in the non-flow of nothing. And then finally the pattern complete: the managers could cough and dust off their costumes one last time before diving into the critical mass of the meeting.

"There's been a lot of talk for some time now about our Japanese competitors and how their parts have been getting better and cheaper with each passing year." Pause, a cough, another dusting. "Well, it seems our competitors have at last finally won."

So the Japs had won. At least a relief for Steve to hear it come from their mouths. The plant manager's. They usually hemmed and hawed. Beat the poor little fucker around the bush until no one cared whether or not the poor little fucker was dead or not. But this time they'd come to the punch with hardly a warning. And it was bad news. And their hands didn't even seem bloody.

Steve watched the flapping yellow tag as the flapping gums of the Head Clown went yammering on about how and why it could be that the Japs had kicked the company square in the chops. The tag kept slapping and the heat grew warmer. But Steve knew it wasn't a raised thermostat. Or an addition of warm-blooded employees. No one else had entered and no one dared make a movement. Certainly not to walk to the thermostat and turn the dial. The humans rolled eyes over nothings in particular. An occasional foot rubbed at a black streak on the tile. And the plant manager's yammering gums, of course. But certainly nothing more. The tag, though, the tag was all-moving. A constant. A fresh familiarity for Steve to sink his eyes into.

"And it is with the deepest regret for me to inform you that Green Tree has been bought out."

A near collective sigh. Some voices in protest,

others in disbelief. Steve scanned the room then shot a glance at David King. But the engineer was staring and Steve followed it back to the flapping yellow tag. So Steve hadn't been the only one watching the caution-colored paperboard dance. And he decided the best thing to do at that moment — that moment of confused voices, clashing, intertwining — was to zone out, let it all fall away and focus on nothing but that stupid slapping tag. And David gazed at it, too. The first thing, maybe the only thing Steve could find that the two had in common. Aside from the everyday. The sleeping and eating and shitting. But then shitting made him remember the time when the black fucker wouldn't shake his hand.

"The company's still deciding on what to do about your jobs. I mean, you're all trained for the job anyway and that would be a benefit, but I can't guarantee that they'll hire anyone on. Or everyone, rather. Certain departments would be phased out, but new ones would be developed as well."

Yellow flapping against cream-colored metal and falling back to dangle for a second above the heads of those sitting in the chairs at the tables. And those in the chairs animated, waving arms, pointing fingers at the middlemen. The middlemen moving lips and tongues and jaws above the ties against buttoned-up dress shirts. And the dustless brown shoes below them. Not part of the costume. An indication to the lie, making the sad and tired only more sad and tired.

"One thing's sure. There will be a lot of changes."

But not the balls to say LAY OFFS. He knew it and so did the rest of the clowns. Steve knew it. David knew it. They all must've had an inkling. Even the yellow slapping tag knew, only it didn't care so it didn't count. And apparently none of the dirty hands clenched and thrust under the pits of those leaning against the walls counted either. They weren't bloody, certainly not bloody, above all blame. But dirty. Graphite traces from hair in disarray down to bootlaces, broken and frayed. And being dirty was a bad thing because it meant the middlemen wouldn't touch them to help them. And the Big Wheels? They hardly knew they existed. And surely ants the country over had their nests, their colonies tunneled through yards and under shops and over graves on great big hills. But they hardly knew they existed, either.

Steve could no longer bear the tag's dance. He looked out the window across from him, over the heads of the workers twitching and coughing and shuffling in place. One great sheet of glass, a divider, another sheet of glass, divider, down the line until the front wall. But there was nothing out there, nothing outside except the cold wet struggle of winter, from the first window to the last. Melted snow on the greenery. Filling the glass nearly to the ceiling. And somewhere in the distance cars passed each other at the bottom of a little valley. Steve could hardly see them. Ants, maybe, bearing the tools and equipment needed to tunnel through the town, the county, the graves, shops and yards. And the anthills running along the road, belching out plumes of smoke, or else lying docile and dormant. The whole land out there full of ants no one would bother to see. Too busy watching the clowns strangle on patterned nooses, spouting spume from worn, red faces.

But then there was David King. Steve turned his head and caught him staring out the window. Arms folded, eyes hardly moving. Maybe he'd spotted an ant far away, performing ant tricks up and down the ant trail. Could've told the managers, could've told everyone in the room of the insects' existence. Then maybe the managers could've fallen on their knees, stained their costumes in the mud and grass, and told the fat turning Big Wheels that they saw them, too. Then they all would've understood the ant squeak as a distinctly sad, sad sound and maybe relieved the ant of its unnoticed anguish. But just an ant after all, and engineers like David King weren't supposed to care too much. Certainly not voice their opinions. Their brains and tongues only useful when the middlemen and the Big Wheels had their ears properly tuned. That is, when opinions were asked of them. And Steve assumed that he hadn't been asked a damn thing. So David unfolded his arms, put them behind his back and watched again the flapping yellow tag.

"I put in my resignation earlier this morning." Pause and sounds of surprise. "But I'll stay on as plant manager until the takeover is complete, so no need to worry."

But why worry? Close enough to retirement anyway. But a good number of those along the walls, at the tables had some years to go. Some were even young and just had kids or got married or took out a five-year loan for a brand new truck. Mortgages to pay, groceries to buy, checks for college to send in come Fall. But these concerns were understood. The middlemen had the same problems. The difference was that they were only concerned about their problems. Anything the workers worried about went unnoticed by the managers so long as it didn't make their lives uncomfortable. Didn't make their jobs harder. But none of it mattered anyway because the shop was sold and they couldn't stop any of it. The Big Wheels would just turn it over to the new Big Wheeled masters and wash their hands even though there wasn't any blood. Besides, why be concerned over the rasping of ants?

The yellow tag stopped. It just hung limp. Steve watched it still, hoping it would move. But he knew it wouldn't until the heater kicked back on to stabilize the cafeteria's temperature. And the temperature just then was fine so why would the tag need to move? Nothing was happening, no heat flowing, so why require a gauge to measure it? No need and so Steve let his eyes slip from the useless yellow tag and fall onto the face of David King. He'd dropped his gaze from the same dead object. And then he turned that severe gaze on Steve and Steve couldn't help but stare back. Into those deep, searching eyes soon melting into liquid glass. And Steve followed further, down inside the rivers that poured from the sockets, splashed through cavities to wash against a big, pulsing brain. And from the brain came a sound atwitching and soon, once again, the gray pulsing lump turned to watery glass and Steve saw what was buried deep within: a yellow flapping tag.

"James, do you have anything to add?" Eyebrows raised, a reluctant head nod. "So now I'll turn the meeting over to Mr. Tudor." And James stepped forward, coughed and dusted his sad, clown jacket.

But Steve knew that the thing had been done. All really over now. The little man in the gray suit and blue tie who had stepped forward couldn't add anything of substance. At least nothing for Steve to bother with. So he glanced at David again, watching the yellow tag in flapping resurrection. Then at the near-final gasp of winter. Other people in the room gazed upon the damp world, too. And Steve could feel the other hardworking souls trapped in the cafeterias of the many shops fanned out from the building Steve and Ted and Ozzie and Dave and Donnie worked at, gazing out their windows onto a soggy reality, cold and bitter, mindless of the ants scurrying to prepare a fresh underground network for the coming Spring. And all these other shops with their own special meetings served only as buffers for the Big One ready to drop on the company with a mighty splat at the week's end. And the Big Wheels turn to squash the ants and say they're sorry. The same as every year. But this one would be different because this would be the last one. Truly the Big One.

And the gray-suited, blue-tied guy just went on. Maybe pretending or maybe sincere. No one listened in any case. They all looked at their feet or through managerial heads or past the glass barrier and the snow-covered hill where, just over the crest, down a steep decline into a shadowed valley, raced their dreams and futures with the speed of screaming jetliners. But the screams would be quickly hushed and life would continue. And the ants would repair the damage to their tunnels. And the Big Wheels would keep on turning. And the engineers would fold their arms and think about the prospects of distant shops in not-so-distant lands. And the echo from the crash of the screaming jetliners would be all forgotten.

But the little yellow tag would flap on.

Little more than a year had gone by since that fateful meeting. A lot of things had changed. Not so much with Steve, personally. Some minor adjustments, a few pinched pennies, not so many pizzas during the workweek. And Steve looked the same. Maybe more grays, but no one could tell and he usually kept his hair crammed under a baseball cap anyway. Still the same shape and size and smell. A working man. A clean working man who sometimes got dirty. But he'd wash himself and look the same old Steve. He even wore the neatly trimmed moustache most guys in the past shop had sported.

But hardly anyone in the made-over shop wore a moustache. Too dorky and old-fashioned. Meant for old people. And not many old timers worked in the new shop anymore. Most of them had gone away to find other jobs in other shops. Some simply retired. New blood, that was it. New blood coursed through the Japanese-owned company and the old blood only hindered the flow. Just clots. But why should Steve care about that? He still got paid in American dollars and American dollars went a long way when pinching pennies.

And he pinched pennies for a reason. His hourly wage had been cut by eight dollars. Eight dollars! That was more than what the new guys started at. But Steve had earned a lot of raises here and there over his twenty-eight years of employment and some of them big ones in the times when the old company had been steamrolling. Used to be something once. They'd been King Shit. But now Steve had to make due on less and not complain because he just didn't have the time.

Another thing that had changed. His time. Cut to a measly lungfuls of breath between cycles. And five cycles now because one operator ran five presses. And the cycles fifteen minutes a piece, leaving three minutes for each press to be unloaded, reloaded and the parts punched out. And six operators per shift. Thirty presses now instead of two, all set in rows, in its own department in the new addition tacked onto the building several months ago. And these new presses were much smaller. Superpresses to be precise. And to think that Steve and that fat load Mac had laughed. These powerful little sonsabitches squeezed out every second of every minute of every hour of every day of Steve's hustling and bustling week, week to week into months and months. No more monitors to watch, no more walls to lean against. And no more bullshit sessions thanks to the stranglehold on time. Wouldn't have mattered if there had been because there wasn't even Mac. He'd gotten out early.

So had others. Ted and Ozzie and Dave were gone. Donnie and that whiney runt Sammy had stayed, but in other plants. Steve hardly knew anyone. And those he did know had only really been acquaintances in the past. Breaks were miserable. Lonelier than hell. Didn't matter that the new middlemen cracked down on lunch breaks going so long because Steve couldn't bear the new people and the new laughs and the new conversations in the freshly-painted cafeteria. He'd always cut them short, push out the relief operator, jump back into the hustling and bustling of his week.

The middlemen walked about more now. Before they'd sometimes make a pass around the shop or tail an abuser of the system like big fat Mac, but usually they'd opted to hide and hole up in unspotted offices. But these new middlemen, they were always in people's faces, shaking hands, pointing out problems or making suggestions, flashing great whites and the sparkling ties flashing with them. And David King now, too, because he'd made plant manager four months after the takeover. He'd flash his teeth and they'd be brightest of all, outshining every middleman in the company. The pale-faces couldn't compete with the white-bright in the deep pink and the surrounding jungle-black of his face. Nor with the princely charm, the cool and collected poise of a friendly cobra.

And Steve kept on hustling and bustling with hardly time to breathe and no one to talk to, knowing all the while that the strong, dark figure of David King strode somewhere in the shop, maybe behind the corner, spying and charting and nodding his head at all the huff and puff before a flicking tongue. But Steve could deal with it because he had to deal with it. Still building up his 401K. And only six more years to an early retirement. And he still had his benefits, so it wasn't so bad. Or at least as bad as it could be. Six more years until freedom in a boat on a lake fishing for bigmouth bass and tipping back cans of Coors Light. Six years then stop, kick back and not even remember the frantic pace of Superpresses. And a hell of a lot more time than three minutes to breathe.

In the future. All in the future. For now a press opened and Steve had to hold his breath and get back to work.

In the early drip of April, Steve stood on his front porch with a coffee in hand. The steam from his mug rose then mingled with the drizzling haze hanging all around. Everywhere was gray: the sky, the distances left and right, the houses across the road. Even the road itself seemed only a darker gray, ripping under and through the mass of airy desolation that tried in vain to squash it. And so hazy that Steve could barely see the grass spread before the houses. And the houses had no features save those roused from memory. Shutters around windows beside front doors. All one confused smear. One wide grayness enveloping the world in its bland yet many-layered raiment.

Steve's thoughts much the same. On a Saturday morning during early Spring nothing of substance pierced bone. Just a dull, thick, lazy fog gently swirling in skull-shaped patterns. And these nothing thoughts, this general mash of swamp-mist stew, would continue on and on until the first brave buds burst from trees and flower beds. But it was early, yet. Not much room for anything but haze and rain. And the haze and rain in his head always tried to leak out his nose and ears to mix with the greater force in the air. Sometimes the channels would reverse and the flow would whisk its way back into the cracks and holes in the head, collecting almost to the point of eruption, then vent in thin, cool streams out the nose and ears again.

And yet Steve unaware as unaware could be. He just sipped his coffee. Straight-lipped, vacant and unaware of staring. The bitterness of the generic brand passing with each sip. Yes, he bought generic brands now, whenever possible, of just about everything. Been tightening his belt for quite a while, despite the persistence of his basketball-shaped stomach. And he wasn't about to spend his Saturday afternoons clipping coupons. He didn't even get the paper anymore. Didn't need it. Just told the same old story. So he'd cut it loose.

Every now and then, roaring beasts would take form from the gray, swirling fog. Dull metal noses that looked wet and cold. Steve watched them leap into the ephemeral fame of the road's center then quickly leap once again into the gray that was their home. And soon the roars would be swallowed, too. And sometimes the beasts would materialize simultaneously, zooming toward one another at near-blinding speed. Then just before the catastrophic crunch and shatter they'd veer and pass in roars, raking all down the sides, almost chipping paint, rending metal. Steve sipped coffee and watched the metal monsters at play, waiting for two to square off and ram each other. One slinking into the fog in disgrace. The other declared alpha male. And Steve would see it all. Merely a spectator. Maybe a spectator among spectators. Some long, strung-out coffee-sipping audience on porches along the route. But they were invisible if present for the gray obscured all. Everything but the three-second glimpses of the roaring beasts. And the flat, depthless charcoal gray shapes among the swirling fog. But even this was too much for Steve. Far too much credit. Nose and ears leaking and he just sipped and waited for a great big wave of destruction to blow him off his porch.

The phone rang from the dining room. He'd cracked the front door because he'd left the keys inside and hadn't been in the mood to deactivate the lock. It was faulty and a real pain in the ass to work. He needed to replace it, but for a while he hadn't the money and then forgot about it until he went to use it and eventually just grew accustomed so that he wasn't going to replace it after all. The ringing again. He turned away from the swirling, roaring stage and pushed through the storm door to answer the phone.

"Yeah . . . uh huh . . . yeah, my wife and son . . . I'm heading there right now."

Steve down the hill of his backyard and into the truck in a flash. He whipped out of the driveway, blew by

Bad Adolph and his sheepish mug and screamed up the wrong-way of the VFD, ignoring the taillights of cars in reverse. A car pulled off the main route and slid down the parking lot toward Steve, but he just gave it the gas and waved the guy out of the way. Red angry face and fingers clutched to the steering wheel. Steve hardly noticed. Unaware as unaware as unaware can be. He didn't stop at the edge of the main route, instead making a quick left-right and leaping onto to center stage, maybe giving someone on a porch a show in three seconds if a car tore through the gray curtain. But no one came and so he swung into his lane, crushed the accelerator and muttered goddamnits between clenched teeth.

All this because somewhere far away someone he knew had met a blind metal beast with the crunch and shudder catastrophe. And he'd missed it because it happened outside his sphere. But he went to check the damage, oh yes, and find out just how glad he was to have missed the initial collision.

All the world streamed by. Barely recognized. Shapes with tracers and traces of color to mark the passing of an object. But it was Steve who moved. Some of the objects moved, too, but none quicker than lightning. And Steve zoomed faster than any natural storm. Faster than any flash and fury rending the sky in ear-bleeding booms. But his truck didn't boom. It roared. And it roared the whole way to the hospital until he cut its throat in the parking lot.

And out and running. A remarkable thing since Steve didn't run anymore. Hadn't the reason or the energy. But today he'd all the reason he needed and enough energy to push one chubby leg in front of the other. Sweat broke out on his forehead and dripped down his face. Armpits and back damp. Slicker than shit and slipping through automatic doors, stopping at the front desk in deep, heavy pants. A few moments before his mouth could work.

"I'm looking for a Kevin Shaw."

The nurse searched through paperwork, but couldn't find the name.

"How about a Joan Archer?"

She found it almost immediately. Room 206. Steve had to go to her if he wanted to find his son. The path to the left, down a hall to the elevators. That's where the nurse's finger had pointed. So Steve followed it until he pressed the elevator button with his own finger. Then he stepped on, hit another button and waited as the doors closed. The elevator was empty. Nothing in it except Steve, cheap red carpeting, flat wooden railings and stale hospital air. His reflection, too, off the polished metal of the doors. Steve watched the blurry image until the doors opened at the first floor to admit a pair of chatting nurses. One held a clipboard to her chest while the other kept glancing at her watch. Nothing special to look at, so Steve gave only the cursory glance at their asses before staring back at his blurry body, splashed against a silver backdrop. Then the door opened onto his floor and he stepped out. The doors closed behind him. Alone and collecting his bearings.

He walked down the hall to the nurses' station. Past that and counting down the numbers to the rooms that held the sore, the sick, the broken and battered. Numbers, numbers once again, but this time not for cheery pictures on lawns beside mailboxes for holiday greetings. Numbers not for individual claims to plots of land with fat smoking houses in the background. Numbers not for mail or pizzas or monthly sports magazines. These people were here to heal. To be tested and eventually set free. The numbers only marked temporary asylum. The numbers hollow and impersonal and stretched with crisp white hospital sheets. Lonely numbers. Letting out the rooms for company. To not be so alone. To be fully realized, important, happy numbers.

Steve found it and stopped. He peered into the

room and saw his ex-wife lying on the bed, eyes closed. He quick-scanned the area. No sign of his son, so he pulled back, waiting behind the comforting shield of the hospital wall. Her eyes had been closed, she hadn't seen him. But if they'd opened, Steve wanted to be invisible. At the least, hidden. And he continued waiting with one arm across his chest and the other propped under the chin. The nurses' station down the hall a bit. He could go back and ask the lady where his son was. He felt stupid in his criminal pose. But he had to hide.

At that moment a nurse passed him, walking by the lonely numbers above the lintels. Steve reached out an arm and almost called to her. But she kept walking because Steve hadn't called to her and Steve hadn't called to her because he caught sight of his son at a vending machine, well past the sphere of the nurses' station. He made his way toward the vending area, not far behind the nurse's heels, until she ducked into a side room. Maybe she'd been sucked in. Maybe the numbers demanded fresh victims. But not Steve, not yet. He kept going until he came to the dusty side of a pop machine. His son looked up from a crouch.

"Hey, you're here," he said.

"How come you're not in a room on a bed?"

"Oh, I'm all right." His son got up, a full can of Pepsi in hand. "Hardly felt a thing."

"So why's she in there?" Steve thumbed over his shoulder.

"You know how she is."

Steve dropped his arm. "All too well."

His son cracked the can of pop.

"You're drinking Pepsi?"

"Yeah."

"What, is the Coke out?"

"No." He took a chug. "Just felt like a Pepsi."

"Pepsi tastes like shit," Steve said. "Too sweet and flat."

"Yeah, yeah, I know." His son shrugged. "But what are you going to do?"

Steve shook his head, hands in pockets. "I don't know, Kevin, I'd almost swear you were turning into one of those Commie pinko pussies." He smiled.

Kevin pointed the can at Steve. His mouth full of effervescence so he couldn't reply. But it didn't matter because Steve would've cut him off anyway.

"So what the hell's going on? The State boys said you were both in an accident."

Kevin swallowed and blinked tears from his eyes. "We were." He coughed then swallowed some more.

"And?"

He shrugged. "Well, I'm OK. They checked me out, but I felt fine. Wasn't sore or anything so I just hitched a ride with Mom on the ambulance."

Steve fishing in his pockets for change. "What happened?"

"Some guy ran a red light at the top of 322—you know, where the bank is and Burger King."

"Yeah, across from the mall." Coins in hand.

"Right, well, that guy hit the person in the intersection and then crashed into us at the light."

Steve rooted around the copper and nickel in his palm. "You got a dime?"

Kevin searched his pockets. "Hit on Mom's side—in the front at an angle." He described the angle with his free hand then pulled out a quarter, handing it to Steve.

"Only need a dime," Steve said.

"That's all I got."

Steve shrugged and turned to plunk the change into the slot. He hit the big red Coke button.

"Yeah," Kevin said. "Took her out on a stretcher."

"And moaning the whole time." Steve bent over to grab the deposited can.

"Of course, worse than ever."

Steve looked at his son.

"Well, OK," Kevin said. "Not any worse than before, but definitely hamming it up."

Steve sighed, standing up. "She always was a whiner." He popped the Coke and drank it down. He let out a healthy belch. "Now that's a man's soda."

"Whatever you say, Dad."

Steve took another swig. Kevin finished his, crushed the can and threw it in the garbage against the wall.

"So what's the damage?" Steve asked.

"Oh, not too bad. The front's a little fucked, blew out a headlight, but for the most part it's OK." Steve polishing off his Coke so Kevin went on. "The car that got clipped in the intersection really got messed up, though. Spun like a top and just stopped right there under the light."

"Jesus."

"Yeah, there was shit all over the road. Weren't even finished cleaning it up when I hopped on the ambulance."

Steve crushed his can, took aim and tossed it at the garbage. It bounced off the rim and clattered on the floor.

"Aren't you going to pick that up?" Kevin asked.

"No, they got people for that."

Kevin shook his head, bent to pick up the can and flipped it into the garbage bin. He stood and faced his father. They looked at each other in silence a while then looked away. An orderly walked between them and bought himself a Coke. He gave Kevin and Steve a glance and a nod before leaving.

"Well," Steve said, facing the pop machine. "I'm glad you're all right."

Kevin nodded. "Yeah, thanks. I feel good."

"Well, good."

More silence. Steve turned around and made his way to the edge of the recessed area, scanning down the

146

halls. A couple of nurses, but nothing more. He looked back at his son, getting himself another Pepsi. Steve shook his head and scanned the halls again.

"So, you want to see Mom, or what?" Kevin asked.

Steve's head snapped back. "Not really."

"Come on." His son led him down the hall toward the room.

Numbers in reverse until the fated 206. Steve peeked inside the sterile cave and slipped back out, thankfully, behind the wall. Her eyes still closed. Kevin stood in the middle of this space, not caring what or who saw him, glancing between a supine mother and a vertical dad.

"She's sleeping," Steve said.

Kevin continued to stare into the room.

"Looks like you two made up."

Kevin turned. "Yeah, a little while back. We're not perfect yet, but you know."

Steve peeked into the room again. "So where's . . . what's his name?"

Kevin's face reddened, eyes to the floor. "Choking on shit, hopefully."

"Uh huh." Steve looked into the room again but this time her eyes were open. "Damn."

"What?" And Kevin turned his head.

She waved and mouthed something weakly. Steve couldn't make it out, but knew it was a summons to enter the room. Her hand poked with an IV, but she waved it anyway. Maybe she'd chosen that hand on purpose. It made the whole request that much more pathetic. And she did look pathetic. But the sad dry eyes were too much. Always were. They had to go.

"Yes, yes, good to see you," Steve said and offered a wave of his own.

But she kept mumbling with those half-paralyzed lips.

"I think she wants you to go in," Kevin said.

"I know." He looked at his son. "I'm fine right here. You go in, I'm going to get myself another Coke."

"Aw, come on, don't be a pud."

Steve's head pulled back. "Excuse me?"

"Here." Kevin held out his pop can. "Take my Pepsi, I don't want it."

"Fuck that shit."

And the lips kept trembling, trying to say something. Maybe they were. But Steve couldn't hear it so he just chose to ignore it.

"I'm fine, fine," he said to the lips. He threw out a final wave, spun on his heels and walked back down toward the vending machine.

Kevin had disappeared into the room.

Steve traced the advancing numbers again, but didn't bother to look into the rooms. Their little secrets could remain their little secrets. He didn't have the patience to deal with the sick, battered and broken if he didn't have to. Hated to see people cry, too, and that's sometimes what you saw when you gazed into a stranger's hospital room. Or else balloons. God, he fucking hated balloons. But more than that, the crowds that always gathered around the balloons. And even more than that, hospitals. He hated them the most. So depressing. Or affectedly cheerful. Better left as secrets.

He had to wait behind a guy who was buying a pop. Looked like a doctor. But he'd selected Welch's grape so Steve knew he must be a fag. That and the gel in his hair. A stethoscope around his neck and dark circles under the eyes. So a fag and probably hitting the drug supplies pretty hard, too. The doctor retrieved his grape soda and just blew by Steve. Didn't even say hey or nothing. Wasn't like he seemed busy or anything if he'd time to grab himself a pop.

Steve shook his head, stepped up to the machine, punched the Coke, chuckling. Grape soda. He stooped then got up with a groan. A pain in the groin area. Maybe his bladder. But he didn't have to piss so he didn't know what the hell it could be. He pressed against it a couple of times and winced. He hobbled over to the wall, leaned his back against it and popped the can. Catching his breath. Eyes closed and twitching. He drank a little and felt the familiar carbonated burn in the throat. Eventually the pain went away, so he pushed from the wall, walking carefully to the edge of the vending section. Then a glance back at the wall. The first time he leaned against a wall since the old days at work. A good feeling. Or had been. And while he stared at the wall, remembering better days, another hospital worker shuffled up to the pop machine. Sure getting a lot of use today.

Steve headed down the hall, drank his Coke, ignored the numbers on high. And mid-sip a nurse came out of the room Steve knew to be 206. She wasn't so bad looking, not from far away at least. A little young maybe, but not too young. Not a teenybopper with Katy Perry popping bubblegum in her head. She headed toward the nurses' station. Steve slowed his pace.

Nobody else at the station. Just her. And she stood in front of it so there wasn't that waist-high wall to bother with. No barrier. No sense of division to mark the space he walked in as out of bounds. So he walked right up to her, past room 206, without looking in, and stopped not far from her side. She wrote something down on a clipboard on the counter. Must've seen the shadow fall because she turned to look at Steve. Not that she was that much shorter than him. Just enough to be acceptable.

"Oh, hi," she said. "Can I help you?"

"I'm just here with my son." Nodding backward. "Room 206."

"Oh, yes, you mean Joan . . ." Tapping her clipboard. "Joan Archer."

"Yeah, her too."

"So you're her husband then?"

"No," Steve said, smiling. "God, no, not for a while."

Her brows lifted. Steve noticed her nametag. Couldn't help but see it, being pinned above such huge breasts.

"Pattie, that's a pretty name," he said.

"Oh, thank you." She gripped the clipboard to her, covering her nametag, but not all of her chest. Simply too much tit to hide.

"How about you?" Steve asked. "You single."

Nodding. "Well, yes, but really, you're wife's who I'm concerned—"

"Ex-wife."

"Ex-wife, yes." She looked toward the room, down the hall, but no one was there. "Your ex-wife seems to be OK, just waiting for the results from the CAT-SCAN—"

"It sounds good to hear you call her my ex-wife."

"Uh, yeah, and so if everything checks out all right, we can send her home tomorrow to get her—"

"How about you?"

Pattie's eyes narrowed. "How about I what?"

"What are you doing tomorrow?"

She blinked and shook her head. "What's that got to do with anything?"

"Well, I don't know, thought maybe we could go get dinner or something."

Shocked and stammering. The silence awful, so Steve took a big gulp of Coke. Wasn't the wisest thing for him to have done at that moment. His throat already constricted from nervousness, leading to a growing feeling of embarrassment, he was sure. But then he'd taken that gulp and now had to choke that sugar burn down his tube until he felt it slide and fizzle from his chest. Eyes watering, blinking away tears with a pained smile. She licked her lips to say something but it wouldn't come.

Steve coughed. "That is, if you're not too busy."

"Do you think this is an appropriate time to ask me to dinner?" She cocked her head.

Steve shrugged. "Sure, why not?"

"I mean, it's just that your wife—"

"Ex-wife."

"Your ex-wife was just in an accident."

"Yeah, I know." Steve held up his can. "So?" He finished it off.

"It just doesn't seem right."

Steve hunted for a garbage can, found one at the back of the nurses' station. He crinkled the can and tossed it in the garbage with a flat, hollow ring. Then back at Nurse Pattie.

"Made it," he said.

"That's great." Pulling away her clipboard to glance at it. "So, it looks like your son's all right, though, that's good."

"Yeah, yeah, that is."

Steve glanced back at 206. His son stood in the doorway with arms folded. He started waving to Steve when he noticed him looking in his direction.

"Well, I really must be going," Nurse Pattie said.

"Yeah, OK." Still facing his son.

Nurse Pattie slipped past him, ducking beneath the radar, clutching the clipboard against her body to deflect CREEPY OLD MAN glances. But Steve had spotted her anyway and spun to follow her healthy, hurried strides. But he didn't move. Just his eyes and they were enough. She'd turned a second and Steve called to her. She stopped, looking over her shoulder. Still clutching her plastic shield. She didn't say anything.

"So how about tomorrow?" Steve and his smile.

"I'm busy," and she whipped around to carry her pink-pinched body down the hall.

"Dad."

Steve turned his big old grin on his son.

"What the hell are you doing?"

"What's it look like?" Steve walked to the doorway of 206.

"Jesus." His son's arms still folded. "You sure can pick the places to score."

Steve shrugged.

"You coming in?"

"I'm leaving." Hands in pockets and nodding.

Kevin sighed. "All right, then. I'm staying a little while."

"Sure, sure, she's your mother."

Kevin glanced back into the room.

"So, I'm going now." Hands out of pockets. "Good to see you." A smile.

"Yeah." Kevin smiled, too. "Glad you could come around."

They met in the middle and Steve hugged his son. A real hard one. And longer than usual.

"I'm just glad you're OK," he said.

"Thanks, Dad."

And Steve quickly released and walked away.

Come Monday, Steve was back at work, safe in his hot, dry haven from the cold rain pelting the rusted roof above his head. The presses cried out to him, begging him to change their diapers, wipe their asses and throw on some fresh new ones. Over and over, all morning, until one of the little bastards shit itself so badly Steve had to shut it down and flip the light switch, calling the fresh-faced maintenance boy from his poorly lit cave to a land the rest of the shop forgot. And he came bounding, snapping on rubber gloves. Steve had just finished reprimanding a snot-nosed little brat when he turned to meet the boy. And boy he was. Couldn't have been more than eighteen.

"What's the trouble?"

But Steve knew more than this kid what the trouble was. Wasn't his job, though, to go screwing with the presses. The machines, the expensive, shiny babies, were not to be soiled by the mitts of the run-of-the-mill operator. Designated solely for the blessed, sterile and gloved hands of the doctors. And so Steve told doctor-boy the trouble. The kid ran away and returned seconds later, pulling a cart full of tools, all laid out in their perfect little Styrofoam niches. He held a set of Allen wrenches to the light, closed one eye. Steve cracked his neck and walked away, answering the wail of another baby press. And then another and another and another until the first baby was messy and crying all over again. But with one press down, Steve had extra time to glance at the boy tinkering inside baby's guts. Then another cry, another diaper, one more ass to wipe before he'd sneak a peak. This repetition until he felt warm, minted breath at his neck.

"Uh . . . you know where the key to the press cabinet is?"

Steve turned around. "Thought you guys had it."

"We usually hang them by the cabinet, but they're not there."

Steve shrugged. "Hell if I know. Maybe one of your other guys has it."

"Maybe."

The boy walked off, disappearing behind a corner. Steve bent to his perpetual task. Unload, load, start. Wipe, apply diaper, then let it kick and scream. When the cycles came round to the downed press, he stared at baby's organs laid out on the press frame and the cart next to it. Poked his nose inside and sniffed. The familiar smell of hydraulic fluid flooded his brain. All inside the gaping wound, spilled down baby's face and pooled on the floor. Baby was bleeding and embarrassing the rest of the nursery with its need. The sparkling clean shop with drooling, trailing, pooling blood somewhere in the middle.

And Steve could've stanched the flow. Could've mended the hole and reattached a brand new prosthetic limb. Not even that. Just a few new seals. Then slap the cylinder back in place, clean the blood and fire the fucker back up. Would've been so easy. Should've been so. But Steve was stuck in old days when he'd access to the seals, permission to mend the press, time to do the job properly. But the old days were gone. And now Union rules to obey. He pulled his head from the cavity because the kicking baby next to him wailed for its change.

And the warm, minted breath again.

"Nobody's got it."

Steve pushed in the cart to the press and hit the button.

"You wouldn't happen to know who else would have it?"

Steve meant to go to his crying baby a few feet away, but the boy blocked him. Steve just stood there, staring at him.

"I mean, if I can't get in the cabinet then I don't think the press will be able to run."

"Well, no shit," Steve said.

The boy stared at Steve, expecting an answer.

"Why do you expect me to know where the hell it is?" Steve asked. "They wouldn't dare let us lowly operators touch their precious presses." He threw his arms out but the boy just kept staring. He put them down and leaned in. "Look, why don't you ask Mr. David King where they are? He's the fucking god around here. Go pester that nigger about it and leave me alone."

The boy dropped his head, turned around and left.

"Doug!"

A boom behind Steve. And Steve knew whose voice it was, but he didn't turn around. Maintenance boy did, though, and stood beside the wounded and bleeding press with a face dead-white and blinking. The jingling of

154

metal and a set of keys tossed over Steve's head into the boy's gloved hands.

"Get it running," the boom said.

A quick nod and the boy vanished. And then silence. A painful moment caught in the chest.

"Steve."

Steve closed his eyes and opened them before turning around. "Yeah."

"If you want to continue working here, I suggest you be more considerate of your fellow employees."

Steve didn't say a word. He didn't blink either.

"I'm writing you up for this." The big, black, hard-lined face. "Don't let me hear you talk that crap again."

Steve still silent. Eyes wandering to the side.

"Get back to work."

Steve waited for the beefy frame of Mr. David King to pass. He picked up a web to place on the cart with shaking hands. The press loaded and he slowly went to the next one. His legs seemed rubbery. Maybe they'd collapse. But Steve kept it together long enough to load another press and move on down the line. He glanced back at his machine out of commission. David King there now and talking and the maintenance boy nodding his head. Maybe his hands shook, too, but Steve couldn't tell. Only a guess. But guessing in this case was probably closer to the truth than not. Steve watched David King's tall body back away and head down the shop, finally fading among the machinery in the distance.

Steve loaded the next press. He moved on to the next one. His hands still shook.

Almost nine months had passed before Steve's next run-in with David King. Not at work. Not in person either. Over the phone, thankfully.

Steve walked out of the Giant Eagle with hands full of stretched white plastic. Heavy, to be true, but he knew they'd hold and so he waddled his way to the shiny red truck. He'd just washed it. The underside still wet. The rubber seals around the windows as well. But the rest of it was dry. Bone dry. And the day dry, too, and windy. Steve squinted when sudden gales cut across his eyes in thin razors. Paper flapped under a wiper. He ignored it for the moment, opening the passenger door to throw the groceries on the seat and floorboards. The door closed and walking around the front of the truck to retrieve the piece of paper.

A horn blared, but it wasn't for Steve. Some woman with a carriage backed into the gap between two cars. Protests silenced, the truck waited until she cleared away then heaved forward, pulling down the lane toward the exit. The woman peeked out the nose of the carriage, timid and shooting glances both ways. Then toward the store with a slight limp and the carriage dragging a rear wheel in front of her. For some reason Steve thought it funny. Sad, too. He didn't laugh. Just smiled and turned around.

The wiper lifted and grabbing for the paper, but the wind snatched it away, sending it scraping across the cruel asphalt wasteland. Then after it, slow at first, soon faster once he realized the damn thing outpaced his fastest walk and so he had to run. It disappeared behind a car. He stopped to look around. The white fluttering again, further down now, and he tore after it. Another honking horn and the paper sailed safe and cozy into shadows. Steve looked at the car in front of him. In the middle of the lane and the driver waving for Steve to get the hell over to the side. Steve nodded, put up his hand and backed out of the way. It rumbled past and he watched it go, but then remembered the paper, walking briskly to the vehicle it had slipped under. To his knees and peering into the darkness then dropping to an elbow. That's when the pain hit. He rolled over. A minute to breathe. On his ass, rubbing at the spot where his bladder burned. Eyes squeezed tight. A coughing fit, a wad of spit into his fist. He collected himself, coughed a couple more times before wiping his hand on his pants. Finally, eyes opened to a world coming back into focus by ever-lightening degrees.

"Jesus."

No cars or people passed. A great relief for Steve as he sat between strangers' cars, stealing ragged gasps of air. At least buffered from the wind. Didn't have to worry about it snatching away his breath as it had the piece of paper. And the cool, smooth sides of autos lent him a temporary sense of protection. From terrorists' missiles and friendly fire. Earthquakes of wrenching asphalt, tsunamis of heavy metal, exclamations as volcanoes from the mouths of a concerned and curious audience. Safe from all that. Or felt so, for the moment. But soon the heat and reek of the world beyond the cool and smooth protecting sides would come to him, forcing him to move, get up, brush himself off and mumble excuses to the deaf and unwrenching asphalt. And, indeed, voices floated to him, slipping from the polished walls.

"OK."

He rolled to peek under the car again, scanning tire to tire, but he couldn't find the paper anywhere. One more look than standing up, wiping the dirt from his clothes and finally circumventing the vehicle. A couple passed and he nodded. They simply gazed upon a man who'd seemed to rip through some car-blocked crack in the pavement. But he kept nodding until he came to the next vehicle in line. Back on his knees, spying again. There it was, caught between a rear tire and flapping its helpless display. So he'd gotten the wrong car. But now he hadn't because the damn thing smacked itself silly against dirty rubber. He reached for it. Too far. Had to crawl in to get it. And he did, quick as possible before someone found him face-first in the oil-spots and bubblegum.

Then up again and glancing at the handwritten lines on the paper. He hadn't read it yet. Not closely. The shelter of his own truck was what he needed now. And so he strode past all the cars he'd run by only minutes before. He stopped at his truck, leaned against its side, reading the paper. A little silence then a growing heat in the cheeks. He stormed to the truck's rear and stared agape at the smashed taillight, the crumpled fender.

"Goddamnit."

The word barely uttered yet shrouded in a caustic mist. Threatened to eat away his teeth and then the paint on the truck. He crushed the paper into a ball and leaned in for a closer inspection of the damage. Torn bits of foamed ram all wedged in a cavity. He snapped to, whipped the paper ball at his back window.

"Goddamnit."

Louder this time. Not as much acid. Venting steam and a searing frustration that just wouldn't bleed off. He clenched his fists and shook in place.

"Goddamnit!"

His eyes opened. A lady who'd stopped loading groceries into her hatchback stared at him. Steve released his fingers and the blood-red cooled to white then flooded back with pink. The frustration grew, forming hair-brained plans of revenge. Several possible avenues more bloody than probable. The logistics of stuffing a head into a press at work too many for his simple mind to work out. Even if the pop of eyeballs, the fizz of meltdown cooled his wrath. Or a hundred other mutilations. A man he didn't know suffered the greatest torments since the Holocaust inside the quaking shell of his skull. And he'd already forgotten the name so he climbed into the bed and got the paper. Back against the cab, unrolling the ball.

"Sun King."

And now Steve's arm dropped to his leg, hand clutching the note, wind making the thing vibrate. He looked up and watched the wispy white smears on the blue sky hardly move.

"Couldn't be a relation."

But Steve didn't know any other Kings in the area. So he just sat there, blank face to the horizon, in the bed of his truck, while all life went by. The cries from birds and engines and babies in back seats before the thunk of closing doors slipped in and out of his head, sailing away into the dry, blue frontier. Maybe mixing with the bigger gusts. Charting flights toward the great hurricanes in the stratosphere. Some time in the future to add its chilled pressure in fanning out the tails of clouds.

"Man, this sucks."

He got himself out of the bed, into the cab and out the parking lot to stop, finally, in the backyard driveway. He trudged up the incline to his house, opened and slammed the door, fuming. A picture of himself with a bass he'd caught four summers ago fell from the wall with a crash. At the dining room table he tried to flatten out the wrinkled piece of paper. The phone grabbed behind him and numbers punched from the note. He tried to slow his breaths, but the heart and lungs wouldn't obey. Blood rushed to his face, made his throat swell. The air in the tube coming in jagged bursts.

"Hello?"

"Hello, I got a note from a Sun King?"

"Ah, yes. May I ask whose calling?"

"My name's Steven Shaw. I got a note on my truck this afternoon with this number."

"Steven Shaw?"

"Yeah, why?"

"This is David King. We work together."

"Yeah, I thought the voice sounded familiar."

A pause and then a sigh.

"So what's the damage?" David asked.

"Well, my left taillight's blown out and the fender's all crumpled to shit."

"Yeah, that's what Louis said."

159

"Louis?"

"My son."

"What's Sun King for, then?"

"Nothing, it's a joke."

Another pause.

"Our vehicle got crunched pretty good, too. It'll cost a small fortune to fix."

"Oh yeah?"

David sighed again. "Yeah, Louis sometimes gets in a hurry and doesn't pay attention."

"So what happened?"

"He says he was getting out of the way of a moving cart, but it's more likely he was texting and didn't look where he was going."

"It is pretty windy today," Steve said.

"Yeah, well, he shouldn't have done it in any case and he's awfully sorry about the inconvenience."

Steve shrugged even though no one could see him.

"What was he driving, anyway?" he asked. "I mean, it must've been big to cause all that damage."

"Yeah, it's big all right. An SUV. Cadillac Escalade."

"A Caddy?"

"Yeah."

Steve shook his head. "How the hell can he afford one of those?"

"Well, I'm paying for it."

Steve's turn to sigh. "See, that's what's wrong with kids these days. Get everything without having to work for it and don't appreciate a damn thing."

"Hey, hey, Steve, the car's my wife's. Louis just drives it once in a while. In fact, he was getting the week's groceries, actually helping out a bit."

Steve chewed on a nail. "Well, yeah, I just meant, you know, just speaking in general." Steve coughed. "Didn't mean anything in particular."

"Sure."

"Just a little upset about my truck, is all."

"I understand."

Silence before David speared it in the side.

"Bring in your insurance information tomorrow. We'll straighten this out at work."

"OK."

"Good day."

"Yeah."

And the line went dead. Steve strangled his, too, looking at the corpse a while before setting it on the table. He cracked his neck, breathed deep. The busted picture on the floor. Forgotten all about it. He went to it and squatted. Careful of the glass, he picked it up. A big crack in the middle and several smaller pieces missing, maybe stuck behind the glass still intact. One side of the frame disconnected from the whole, hanging toward the floor. Steve placed it on the table and went to the backroom to get the broom and dustpan. He'd salvage what he could. The body broken and lifeless, but maybe he'd manage to slip out the picture and preserve the soul of the moment on that happy fishing trip far too many summers ago.

It was now a brand new summer. Or just about. The distant gleam then glow then pink to yellow splashes across the late springtime sky. At its end and blushing from the clarity and heat of the coming summer. The second weekend in June. A Saturday. And Steve didn't have to work on Saturdays so he was out fishing. And happy for the moment because fishing always made him happy.

"I think this hole's done," Ted said. "I'm going down a little further to hit another one."

"Wait a minute," Steve said. "I'll go with you."

Steve had already reeled in his line, adjusting the shoulder-strap to his creel. Two ten-inch trout, gutted and on icepacks. He'd caught more than the two of course, but he never kept anything under ten inches. Catch and release, catch and release, catch and release for more times than he could remember. And his old friend Ted did the same. From hole to hole, bend to bend, down the river, through the underbrush and trees, growing thicker and thicker the further the distance from the usual worn paths. And now and then Steve and Ted would come to a big enough hole where they could both stop and fish and catch a good chunk of time shooting the shit.

Ted went a little ways ahead before disappearing into a green tangle. Steve hunkered down and tore himself through the clinging branches and twigs. Once through he saw Ted standing at the river's bank in a good-sized clearing. He walked up beside him. Ted scanned the river up and down and turned to Steve.

"Looks like a good spot," he said.

"Maybe the best hole we've seen all day."

Ted nodded and pointed at a clump of dead branches trapped in the wide bend of the stream. "I'm heading for that."

Steve nodded and rummaged for a nice fat crawler. Ted stepped down the bank a bit and cast his line. The current caught it, carrying it toward the branches. Steve pierced the worm on the barb a couple times then headed down the bank in the opposite direction. He cast his line, too, and watched it make its way to the head of the hole. The sun shined on this spot of the river and Steve followed the light through a clearing of trees. Not a cloud in the sky. Bright, blue and cutting a long slash through the green. Trees hung all around him. Well shaded and quiet. Would be until night decided to swallow up the smaller shadows. Steve breathed in and out and watched the line slowly being sucked into the water's churn. They'd found a good spot. And Steve knew they'd walk away from here with their bags a little heavier.

"I could stay here all day," Ted said.

"Know what you mean." Steve reeling in his line.

The chirp of birds far away and close. All around. The rush of water ever-present. A light breeze tugging at the strands of hair poking from the back of Steve's baseball cap. A pair of dragonflies in the shade to the right, bumping together along the bank then veering sharply, out over the water, into the sun to warm iridescent bodies before shooting back into the shadows of the far bank. And soon Steve had his hook out of the water. He glanced at Ted, calm and steady, slowly working his reel. Steve flipped the worm back into the river and watched it sail into the golden waters at the head of the hole. The birds, the rush, the light breeze tickling his ears, making him smile, almost with the childish urge to giggle. And then the dragonflies came out bumping each other again.

"You hear about Ozzie?" Ted cast his line.

"You mean about him being divorced?" Steve looked at Ted, but Ted only watched the river.

"How'd you find out?"

Steve shrugged. "Ran into Donnie the other day after work. We talked for a few minutes, you know, caught up on old times."

"Sure, sure." And Ted's line drifting into the branches in the bend.

"Everybody knew it was going to happen."

"No great mystery there."

Ted watching the branches still, watching the line. And Steve, too, single-minded and serene, noting the line at the end of its journey, breathing deep, bringing back the bait now, real slow, steady, taking his time, letting the rush of water fill his ears and head then down into his body, through the limbs and their extremities, down to each and every pore. Steve felt alive with the river. Rod-hand buzzing. But it could've just been falling asleep. He stopped reeling a moment so he could flex the fingers of his other hand.

"Saw him downtown a couple months ago," Ted said.

"Who's that?"

"Ozzie."

Steve looked to Ted.

"Yeah," Ted said. "He was at Mikey's with a bunch of guys I didn't know. Dumbass was all shit-faced — kept spitting in my eye and telling me how leaving Green Tree was the best damn thing he ever did."

"As if he had a choice."

"Yeah, Ozzie always thought he was the backbone of the whole corporation for God knows why." Ted scratched his temple, gazing over the water. "This gap-toothed skank was hanging off him and Ozzie was acting like he was King Shit or something."

Steve shook his head.

"Acting like a real asshole," Ted said. "I mean, he was OK to me, but I won't shed a tear if I don't run across the guy again for a few years."

"That's too bad." Still shaking his head. "He could be an all right guy sometimes."

"Getting a little squirrelly near the end there."

Steve sighed and cast his line out again.

"Oh well, things change," Ted said.

But Steve hardly listened. He knew Ted was done. For the moment, anyway. He'd just reel and cast, reel and cast until he caught a bite. Or maybe Steve would. Didn't matter. Not now. They'd get a few hits in before they'd leave this hole because they both knew it to be a good hole and were determined to work it until they snared some loot. And the water's rush gave Steve a sudden urge to piss. But he'd wait it out. Didn't have to go that bad, really. Could hold it until the eventual trek to the next hole. Piss on some tree and listen to the patter on bark and leaves usurp the royal rush of the current, shielded by

164

trunks and the wide-green screen. But for now standing and watching and waiting for the tugs at the bait.

"Think my line's caught," Ted said, the tip of his rod bending as he struggled to free the line.

"Oh yeah?"

"Jesus man." Ted pulled and pulled but the thing wouldn't give. "The damn thing's really stuck."

Pitifully hunchbacked now. Crippled. Ted gave it a couple quick yanks, dipped back down, yanked again. Nothing.

"Come on, man."

"You're going to break your rod if you keep pulling on it like that."

"I know." Ted eased up and took a few calming breaths.

"Looks like you're going to have to go in after it." Steve smiled.

"Fuck that, the water's too deep. I'm not going out there in that shit." Ted nodded toward the bend. "And I'm sure as hell not fighting my way through all that brush."

Raised shoulders. "Looks like you only got one option then."

"Uh huh." Ted nodding.

Steve slowly reeling in his line, watching Ted hold the rod back and grab a hold the line, yanking it one two three before the snap. The rod jumped with the release while the broken line whisked down the river. Ted sat on his ass on shaded grass. The eyelets needing rethreading so there wasn't any point in hurrying himself.

A bird zipped by Ted's head, spinning off into the blue, circling a clump of green just over the river. Then around and zooming its way back to the men on the bank, the last minute cutting sharply to the left, wings over water, and burying itself into the branches above Ted. Another burst, a leaf ripped prematurely from its stout, young limb as the bird tore into the sky. A second bird followed just as fast to disappear somewhere past the drooping crown of a weeping willow. Its bulk, its self-contempt nearly shrouded by the stalwart guardians of the forest. And yet the other trees, the happy trees, couldn't blot it out altogether. The willowy sliver of sadness blew in the breeze; a testament to the darker things the forest tried to hide under brush and leaves and twigs all ajumble. But before Steve could let that solitary plea, that solitary, silent voice sink into his blood, the birds reappeared. Or exploded rather. From all the bright, sheeny greenness and the swaying leafy shadows thrown onto parts of the river and Steve's body. The birds zeroed in. Ted's skull a ripe melon target. They didn't pull up until he threw out his arms in defense. Then a sudden rocketing under the forest's splayed limbs, disappearing once again.

"Holy crap, did you see that?"

And Steve laughing his ass off. So hard he stopped reeling in his line.

Ted's eye bulging at Steve then up into darker and darker tree-limbed depths. "Christ, I thought the things were going to take off my head!"

Steve still laughing, clutching his side. And it only made the urge to piss stronger, but he'd be damned if he could stop.

But soon Ted was laughing, too.

"Man, that one would've been tough to explain to the wife," Steve said.

"She never would've believed it was a bird."

Both laughing a while. And eventually calming enough for Ted to begin threading the line to his rod, sneaking glances into the trees above for any sign of attack. His body shook and he had to give up his task for the moment.

"Can't do this right now, can't stop shaking."

Steve had resumed reeling his line. "Aw, come on now, Ted. You going to let a couple little birds scare you away from fishing?"

"Screw you, man, they weren't coming for your head." Ted rested his pole against his leg. Eyes rolling all around. Face a nervous grin.

"It's like that movie with all those birds attacking people," Steve said. "Maybe it's happening now. Maybe you pissed them of a while back and don't know it and now they're looking to take you out."

"Yeah, maybe."

Ted closed his eyes a few deep breaths. Steve smiled and looked away. The river flowed sure and strong and that made him feel better. Pains from a non-relieved bladder not as stinging. He checked the hook. The bait all right, he pulled back and flipped it into the water. Little laughs escaped him and he shook his head. Flowing with the stream. The line went out nice and easy and Steve felt he could burst out singing if he'd been the kind of person to sing out loud. But he wasn't so he kept his mouth shut while his shoulders shook out the little laughs.

"You hear about Mac?" Ted threading the line again.

Reeling nice and easy and steady. "Mac? What the hell's that fat bag of shit up to?"

"He's dead."

"What?"

Ted threading, avoiding Steve's stare. "Yeah, he was mowing his lawn one day and just keeled over."

"You're shitting me." Steve's grin had dropped and he'd forgotten about his line.

"Couple of weeks ago. Poor bastard didn't even make it to summer."

"How come I didn't hear anything about it?"

Ted shrugged. "I don't know, maybe you don't read the paper."

Steve reeling slow, paying no mind. He gazed into the woods on the other side. Nothing popped out, shook its feathered head, beat its insect wings. Just green and green and more green expanding across his vision, pushing out the blue, above the clear water and its reflections below. Only green and deep and all the individual lines of twigs and trunks, the curves of clouds and heads of trees, every and anything not part of the GREAT BIG GREEN soon melding and washing and spreading out until nothing but the nothing of green became all.

"Wow," he said, eyes full of emerald. "Couldn't last outside of work. Died working. Mowing the lawn and just dropped."

"Yeah, as if Mac ever really worked anyway," Ted said. "Just walked around and made it look like he was working." Ted cocked his head at the river. "In fact, he didn't even do that."

The great wide stretching green snapped and Steve shook his head. A tug on the line. First he felt it, then he saw the end of his rod straining to reach the branches across the stream. "Hey." Another tug and he started to reel in his line. "Hey, hey."

Ted looked up. "You got something?"

"Looks like," Steve said.

His pole bent. He eased off a bit. A couple more tugs before reeling again.

"Well, damnit," Ted said. "I want to play, too."

He'd just finished tying a new hook. Into his bag for a fresh worm. The poor sucker stuck on the cruel barb with haste. Ted stood up and brushed dirt from his ass.

"Think this one's going to be big," Steve said.

Ted rushed to the bank and cast his line. And while the constant river flow carried the crucified worm to a deep, tangled hell of branches at the bend, the birds erupted once again from the leaves, spinning circle after circle in the heaven's shine over the water.

"There they are," Ted said, pointing. "The bastards."

But Steve too busy to notice. Reeling and tugging and huffing and puffing until nearly out of breath and then more reeling, tugging, huff-puff and clenching because he had to pee.

"Man, this son of a bitch is a real fighter," he said.

And Ted, also, far too preoccupied to bother with his buddy's parochial bank-side struggles. The birds seemed to be conspiring in an ever-tightening huddle, plotting to take down the arrogant man with his hooks and bagful of prey. The brave, stupid, proud man who'd dare face the elements, all of nature, in this otherwise peaceful spot in the woods. Crash their beaks into his fat, stupid head and sink into the unprotected bloody lump. Squawking and flapping, waiting for the man to look away so they could launch the attack. And once they'd got that useless load of a man on his back and pecked into chunks, they'd turn reddened eyes, red-black feathered heads full on the other useless load at the other end of the stream.

"Jesus Christ." Ted turned to Steve but Steve wasn't watching. "They're watching me! Their fucking eyes are looking at me, I swear!"

"You're crazy," Steve said. But he still wasn't paying attention. Not really. The tug and the reel consumed him. Any outside noise merely a distraction that needed swatting.

"Holy shit." Ted tightened up. The birds had stopped circling and tore for his head. "These birds are psycho." And he waited to see if they'd pull up. "Steve!"

"What?" He finally turned to Ted, his pole bouncing in his hand.

The first bird came at him, aiming for the sweaty spot between the eyes. Ted screamed and swung his rod around. And yet the bird came on. Its partner, too, cutting through the air, slicing sunrays and splashing the glowing lifeblood all over itself and down into the streaming water. "Ah!" and Ted dropped the rod to the ground and covered his head. The bird missed him by inches but the second screamed toward him with uncanny purpose. And ready to slam its sleek-beaked missile-kiss home.

"Get to the ground!" Steve waving his hand.

Ted fell to his knees then pitched onto his face. Arms up, wrapped around a screaming skull, the bird zipping through, a foot above him, careening and curving in the woods then straight back for him. The first bird had disappeared. Steve had lost all track of where that silent bomb was hanging.

"Jesus Christ." Ted made to get up.

Steve waving and waving. "Stay down, stay down."

His pole tugged again and jerked his head back to the river. He reeled, stealing glances at Ted's prostrate figure. His buddy whimpered and cursed and still the black bird from hell came on.

"It's coming back, Ted, it's coming back!"

But the damned thing pulled a ninety, barreling at Steve with wings flapping on a fuel that burned hotter than the fire in his bladder. And that recent familiarity hit him again. That stinging pain below the belt. But Steve didn't feel the need to piss now. Just to fall to his knees, perform the same prayers and curses his buddy did before filling his mouth full of dirt. And so Steve clutched the rod when the pain struck again. He pitched forward, pulled in his head, scrunched up the shoulders so his forehead pressed against his rod. Silently succumbing to the pain. Hoping the vengeful bird god would be appeased at his show of humility. And then even the thought of the flying bird vanished, squeezed out by the stabbing pain. The greenery, too, replaced by the throbbing dark and blotched redness from his eyes forcing inward. Maybe to protect themselves against the beak zeroing on their wet and streaming helplessness. But the bird's existence had disappeared for Steve. And, too, the green then the dark and red and finally even the white stabbing pain until he opened his eyes. Then a flood of sunshine.

"Goddamnit," he heard Ted say. And then

splashes and swift flowing water.

Steve's focus widened and cooled. The black missile nowhere to be found. Apparently sinking itself into some other unfortunate target past the deep green of the forest. Ted knee deep in the river, hurrying after his rod in the stream. The current slammed against his legs, making him teeter, capering monkey-fashion just to keep from falling.

"I got it, got it!" Ted lifted his pole from the water and performed the same ridiculous monkey dance back up the river.

Steve still on his knees, clutching the rod with red fists. But something was missing. Something felt different. And then Steve realized the tugging was gone. He reeled in his line, but it was hopeless. The big bastard had gotten away, lucky prey. If not for the bird, if not for the pain. But no point in moaning over his loss, so he got to his feet, wiped his eyes and kept reeling. And yet he moaned. Forgetting the pointlessness of it. But low enough so Ted couldn't hear. The vibration in his throat and chest felt good. Seemed to assuage some of the grief over his lost prize. One last moan and it seemed to shake its way to his bladder, giving the swelled balloon a healthy kick. Steve quickly brought in the rest of the line.

"What were you on your knees for?" Ted on the bank, heading toward Steve.

"That damned bird came after me."

"You too?"

Steve shook his head. He stooped to place his rod on the ground.

Ted looked from the rod to Steve. "You lose her?"

"Yeah, she broke free."

And now Ted shook his head, looking behind him at the river, across it into the woods, up and around through sky and trees. He turned back to Steve and smiled.

"I think they're gone now."

"Yeah." Steve nodded, offering a pained smile. He couldn't totally conceal the little spasms and shakes and shifting of feet.

"Maybe we should go on to another hole." Ted glanced behind him again. "Looks like the place is bad luck. Weird voodoo vibe or some shit with those crazy-ass birds and all."

"Yeah."

Ted cocked his head at Steve. "You all right?"

"Yeah." Steve smiled, spasms in the lips and shaking while he tried to keep his feet from shifting.

"I think we should head on."

"Yeah."

Ted pointed at Steve's rod on the ground. "I think you're going to need that."

"I got to pee," Steve said and hopped from Ted, bursting into the woods to find a safe little haven for release.

Ted stood there with a big dumb face and waited for Steve to return. Sometimes shooting glances at the river. Searching the woods for feathered horrors. But then Steve came crashing through the green, tightening his belt and sighing. He had a big dumb face, too, with a big dumb smile to match. Ted picked up his friend's fishing pole.

"Don't forget this," he said.

"Thanks."

One last scan of the forest and Ted led the way along the trail that paralleled the stream. But then the tiny rebellions of a curve or rise or momentary disappearance in the warm suck of the forest's vacuum. Steve right along after, watching Ted's back, sneaking glimpses through the foliage for the suicide bird squad, catching grateful gulps of air, cracking his neck, jouncing on through the brush with the lightness of a jettisoned cargo hold. Over every curve and rise and disappearance of the trail. And the forest opened its trap to swallow Ted and Steve and whoever else was brash enough to amble into thorny jaws.

But, of course, Steve paid it no mind. Just a darkening before the eventual rush of fresh air and light. Maybe swat a bug, bend a branch away from his face. Blind, almost, in the darkness. Then a growing light. Ted bright and golden, breeching the back of the forest's throat, looking back and squinting.

"It's a shame," he said. "That last hole looked like a good one."

"You never can tell."

And now Steve blundering through the trees; arms outstretched, head bowed. He blinked away the light and stopped a moment to let his eyes adjust. Then back into the forest's throat. No blood, no evidence of pain. Just a shredded hole with leafy bits hanging against the darkness within, flapping from a breeze. The forest's labored breaths, having bypassed the lungs. Straight through the tube. A pitiful wheeze, barely. But no pain, no crying out, no blood. Maybe not a throat at all. More of a vessel. One among thousands all wending their way through every cranny and crevice in the wooded seclusion. And then maybe the river its spine. And Steve and Ted had felt perfectly fine dipping their dirty hooks into life-giving fluid, pulling out flailing chunks before laying them out on the river's side, slicing them open with cruel and foreign instruments. So Steve a foreigner. Ted, too. At least in this place. This quiet, private, secret place. Small wonder the forest had sent out its sleek black missiles after them. Infections, both. Inept, irreverent and lucky to have escaped whetted beaks.

Steve patted his bag of gutted fish. He turned around, went further into the clearing to inspect the new view of the river, naked and maybe unaware of the trespassers with their hooks and knives. This hole didn't look as good as the last one. He'd have to make due.

"We stopping here then?" Steve shielding his eyes.

"Sure, why not?" Ted scanning the river. "Looks

all the same to me, anyway."

"Wish we were on a boat on a lake."

"Well, we're not fishing for bass, are we?"

Steve stepped to the bank, rod in hand. "Weren't expecting birds to come swooping down on our heads either."

Ted at the bank, too. He looked at Steve then the river.

"Just more familiar with bass," Steve said.

He flipped his hook into the water. Ted hadn't answered. Probably blanked to speech. Silent and watching the river. And so Steve, too, shut his mouth and gazed over the water, slowly reeling, hoping for a renewed tug on the line.

ALKAHEST

It was a bit warm in the doctor's office, especially on a late June day. Steve noticed the AC wasn't on, or at least couldn't hear the fans blowing. The back of his thighs and ass stuck to the pale blue pleather of the exam table. He pulled on the hospital gown at the neck, but it still clung to him, despite the alternating pattern of big and small snowflakes. Snowflakes. And Steve's feet itched to land on the footstool below, to stand and stretch that wintry landscape, to untie the chokeholds at his nape and waist, to clothe himself in faded blue jeans and a fagged-out tee, to walk straight out the office into the sun and his truck that could blast an arctic breeze before he'd even pull out of the lot.

But the doctor had returned and plunked himself down on the powder blue medical stool and rolled it toward him. Steve didn't fancy being at crotch level to the doctor, so he turned his attention to a poster: PATIENT ALERT. Something about stopping the spread of germs. The doctor scooted closer and was talking.

". . . chronic prostatitis . . ."

Sounded like a term on a worksheet at the plant.

". . . or more properly, chronic pelvic pain syndrome . . ."

Absolute break room fodder.

". . . DRE . . . EPS . . . RPD . . ."

Steve's gaze drifted to a chart of the gastrointestinal system that floated above the doctor's gray head.

"... need a urine sample first, of course ..."

Steve kind of did have to pee.

"... digital rectal examination ..."

And now the piss scared straight out of him.

"... well-lubricated gloved finger ..."

Steve's asshole gripped the pleather.

"... inserted into the rectum ..."

A spiraled winter wonderland.

"... any abnormalities of the gland ..."

Abnormal, like a finger in the butthole.

"... gentle massage of the prostate ..."

Gentle.

"... about four drops of prostatic fluid ..."

Steve slid back and bumped into the diagnostic equipment mounted to the wall. He straightened his gown and pointed a finger. A bent finger. A working man's finger after it had been scrubbed with pumice. A finger free of the scent of shit and shame.

"Doc," Steve said, "you're going to bend me over and make me come?"

The doctor's tired old face dropped. "It's called a prostatic massage. Or milking."

"Go milk a snake." Steve waved his hands. "You're not fingering my ass."

"This isn't funny, Mr. Shaw."

"You bet your ass it's not." Steve crossed his arms. "Or my ass, rather."

The doctor sighed and rolled his stool back a step. Steve shut his mouth, arms still crossed, and gazed at the physician scale to the side. Eye level and inert. And the doctor went on.

"... anti-inflammatory medications ..."

Steve considered the square waste container. Also blue. The bin that would receive a glove uncomplaining. A glove that would stretch along an old man's finger. A glove that would snap and crumple itself into a ball to hide the memory of the probing. Massaging. Emission. Steve felt his stomach flip.

". . . muscle relaxants . . ."

He'd need to be relaxed, all right. And Steve considered the base cabinet with the stainless steel sink. Now dry but soon to be covered with droplets from a washing. After the plunging. The cornholing. No, there was absolutely nothing funny about this. And Steve could feel the cotton suck to him as a protective second skin.

". . . hot baths . . ."

Cold showers.

". . . drinking extra fluids . . ."

Lots and lots of beer.

". . . relaxing when urinating . . ."

Who didn't do that? And Steve considered again the PATIENT ALERT poster and wished to God he'd only had the flu.

". . . ejaculating freely . . ."

Steve turned back to the doctor. "All right, all right," he said. "I get it. Do we have to keep harping on it?"

That tired old face almost seemed to smile. "Well, yes, Mr. Shaw," the doctor said. "I'm afraid we will have to start a regimen — three days a week for at least a month. Maybe longer. We've got to ensure you're fully drained and free of any pressure."

Or some such. Steve was kind of in and out of it, quite frankly. He just couldn't look the doctor in the eyes knowing that this old fart was going to be knuckle deep in his backside as many days a week the Pirates played at home.

"Oh God, butt pirates," Steve said.

And audibly groaned.

"Are you sexually active, Mr. Shaw?"

The doctor cocked an eyebrow, maybe to stop himself from grinning. Steve found it hard to believe that the doctor didn't think it funny. But it wasn't. Flat-out serious shit.

"Not at the moment."

Steve strongly considered visiting a prostitute instead and seeing if she wouldn't mind sticking her painted digit up his posterior three times a week.

"Good," the doctor said. "Than we won't have to check for Chlamydia."

"Chlamydia?"

"Otherwise, after EPS collection, you'd have to have a cotton swab inserted about one centimeter into the urethra for mucosal cell testing."

Or some such. Steve dropped his head and felt like passing out. Stuck to the table. Stuck to the wall. Arms stuck against his chest as the doctor went on and on.

Steve considered the big and small snowflakes. He knew that when he peeled off this sticky fabric, he wouldn't be the same man. Something would be lost. Or taken. There were only two kinds of snowflakes. Those that get poked in the butthole and those that do the poking. The big and the small.

And the doctor told Steve to stand up and turn around.

SMART PHONES AND
DUMBASSES

Later in the week, a day between rectal insertions, Green Tree threw a surprise going away party for their latest plant manager. He'd had the shortest stay of them all, to Steve's memory, but had the biggest impact. Not just because he was black. Not just because he'd transformed the floor from three colossal presses to a battery of fifty running at five times the speed. Not just because they had their first big rash of new hires in twenty years. If you'd come into the break room and counted all the heads and shoulders squished together from wall to wall, there'd be no doubt that this impromptu party was for someone who was anything but impromptu. He was substantial. Stalwart. Taller than everyone. And darker than the round ceramic disks they baked in all those constantly chugging presses.

He was substrate. A foundation. Something upon which a project of import could be built.

And Steve's asshole was sore.

At least the AC was working.

"Not many of us old timers left."

Steve turned to the lady beside him. She was around his age.

"Hey, Carla," he said, suddenly smiling. "How'd they let you in here?"

"Well," she said, "he monitors our plant, too."

"Does he?"

"And already leaving," said Vickie, standing beside Carla. "We're sure going to miss him. Really fixed things up."

"Yeah, well, you weren't here in the 80s," Steve said. "When it was really booming."

"It's booming now."

Steve just shrugged. Across the sea of bumping foreheads he watched Donnie thread his way to a table holding assorted cookies, chips and cans of soda. Steve waved and caught Donnie's eye as he grabbed a silver cylinder of aluminum. Like an obsolete part from one of the ancient presses. Shiny and new and on display as if to show just how far the company had come.

"Don't call him over," Vickie said. "Fuck."

Steve tilted his head.

"They had a thing," Carla said.

"Fucking asshole," Vickie said.

And Steve scratched the back of his head.

Donnie had squeezed his way through the mass and looked thinner for it. Skinnier than Steve had remembered him being. He popped the tab to his soda and beamed at Steve that YOU OLD DOG grin.

"Diet Coke?" Steve said.

"I guess I'm the only one that drinks Diet Mt. Dew." Donnie took a swig. "It'll have to do."

"Diet?"

"Not going to stay young forever," he said. "Got to look good for the ladies."

"Hey, Donnie," Carla said.

"Fucktard."

And Vickie bored into Donnie until he dropped his gaze. Right there on the tiles for anyone to see. Anyone who wasn't so crushed they could roll eyes toward the red-faced shame staining the break room floor.

"So," Steve said, "you all commies in plant three?"

"We're in plant three," Carla said.

"You all work together?"

"That's right," Donnie said. Back up and grinning with arms out wide. "One big happy family."

"Assfuck," Vickie said.

"Jesus Christ, Vickie, that was three months ago."

"Stuff it, Donnie," Carla said. "Just shut your mouth."

"Dickfart."

Donnie shrugged.

All this talk made the back of Steve's pants tighten.

"I'm going to mix a bit," Vickie said to Carla. "Nice seeing you again, Steve."

She pulled an invisible dagger out of Donnie's throat as she walked away. More subsumed than walking actually. Sucked into the greater host body. A many-headed beast with shiny brows and teeth gnashing at air and cookies. Mostly strangers. To Steve anyway. New acquisitions from the ever-expanding girth of the Green Tree bole. Branches thrust into the thickening atmosphere as other newer beings were absorbed into the laughing, chatting, grinning, patting bulk.

"What the hell's up with that stache, man?" Donnie said.

Carla nodding. "I was going to ask the same thing."

"I don't know," Steve said. "Something different."

"It really ages you," Carla said.

"Yeah, you look like a state trooper," Donnie said.

Steve felt his shoulders sag. He was the only one in the room with a mustache. A few beards, goatees. But no one sported a paltry strip of fuzz above their upper lip. No one else wore the t-shirt with the company's old logo. No one else had to have their prostate manually depleted by an old man's shaking finger. And Steve felt like no one else in the room because he was the only one conscious that he was not part of the room-squeezed twitching body. He was apart. Apart and exhausted as his faded out tee.

"Ah, crap."

David King had caught Steve's stare and nodded. Steve nodded back. And then the big black tower turned toward the man slapping his back. Neither man had a mustache, of course. But Steve felt a minor swell of pride at the acknowledgement, nonetheless.

"Well, I'm going to see where Vickie got off to," Carla said.

"I can tell you where she gets off," Donnie said.

Carla's eyes hardened and she pointed a finger. Suspended for longer than necessary maybe. A strong lean digit. Free of grime and polish and shit. Shit. Why couldn't Steve stop thinking about it? And he shifted his feet to separate the cheeks a little.

"Right, right," Donnie said and bowed his head.

A muttered dumbass while walking away. Joining to the symbiotic crush. Donnie, too, now looking uncomfortable to be standing alone with the only man in the room with a mustache. A ridiculous, state trooper stache. Or at least Steve felt it must be, since Donnie surveyed the crowd, hitting the can more times than the thing could've possibly had liquid, hitting it over and over, even when it became obvious that he was only sucking metal. He returned watery eyes to Steve and coughed.

"You know," he said. "I actually do care about her."

"Who?"

"Vickie."

"Oh, oh."

Donnie crushed the can.

"She said her niece really wants a smart phone for her birthday," he said. "But that she hadn't the money to get it. That she was too young for it anyway."

Steve swore Donnie was about to cry.

"You think that would get me back in her good graces, if I got her one?"

Steve opened his mouth. Shook his head. Let the buzz of the room fill up his silence. Something encouraging, he felt, would have been nice. But what could he say? Donnie was part of the host body. An alien from a distant planet. Steve only circled the sphere in outmoded orbits. Up there with the rest of the dead satellites and winkless debris. And the language he spoke was the language of a long extinguished race. Steve wondered what his voice sounded like in Japanese. If he'd been the one sent to Japan or Brazil or wherever it was Mr. David King was being shuttled to. He'd be just as pointless and untranslatable as he was here. So he cleared his throat.

"Fuck if I know," he said.

And went to brave a human avalanche on his way to a soda.

Steve stopped twice on his way home.

Once going up the hill at the curve before the VFD building came into view. The Paki was out again raking, his back to traffic, working in methodical paths toward the white line of the berm.

Steve eased his truck into the pull-off lane and cut the engine. He waited for a moment, allowing cars to whisk by in both directions. At a lull he could hear the scrape of metal on tarmac. The insect chorus in the high grass. A distant airliner cutting white across the blue belly of the sky. His windows open. The radio off. The world all abuzz around him. The chatter from separate beings occupying the same curve of the same hill of the same road in the same township that Steve had lived on for the past thirty years. For as long as he'd worked at the plant. And the high grass before the lot leading to the VFD was only ever cut once a year. It was enough. Off on its own, only fringing the route between neatly trimmed squares. An allowable strip of chaos within the ordered lot upon lot upon lot. And here was this guy raking gravel. Stones that would never stay in place. Like water spilling down a hill during a storm. Ever restless. Ever coursing. Running gutters through soil to wash over and carry away the smaller pebbles at the Paki's feet.

On moaning hinges Steve swung free the door, looked both ways, and pushed it back with a cavernous snap. The echoing ring from a mausoleum door. And he shifted feet across the asphalt, toward the man with his back still turned, arms ceaselessly working. Steve stopped a couple of feet away. Maybe a shadow fell. Maybe a prickling sense of being watched. Maybe the smell of a barbarian in a strange foreign land. A head turned to peer over a shoulder. And the face wore a mustache.

"What's your name?" Steve asked.

"Excuse me?"

Fully turning round now, rake in hand.

"I see you out here all the time, everyday," Steve said. "And I don't even know your name."

Perspiration beaded on the brow, caught in the wrinkles.

"Rakesh," the man said.

"You've got to be shitting me."

The man wiped at an eyebrow.

"Can I help you?"

Steve pointed at the neat little grooves behind the man.

"Why do you always rake the stones in your driveway?"

"To keep order."

"But the order is constantly upset. It rains, it snows, the wind blows."

The butt of the rake to the ground and gripping the handle, maybe to keep the implement from working on its own, so that master and object could toil in unending unity.

"Then you must work harder to regain that balance," he said.

"But what if you can't?"

The man shrugged. A car blew by.

"An ordered house is a happy house."

He shrugged again and returned to raking. Steve

186

just stood and watched him. More cars passed. He meant to say several things. Several attempts stalled. Like a truck without gas. Like rivulets without the flood. Like contrail plumes that dissipate overhead.

"My name's Steve."

"OK."

Without a pause. Without turning around.

"Been a real pleasure, Rakesh."

"Yes, yes. A pleasure."

And Steve spun on grating heels. A barrage of cars blew dust around him. He blinked, heard muttering from behind and knew that some of the stones must've been disturbed. Always would be. Part of the ever-changing but never-changing landscape. Part of the road and curve and township. Nearly ripped out its throat when he threw the door wide. Hopped in and turned the ignition. The sounds of raking and insect chatter and distant planes all lost in the rumble of the beast. He pulled forward.

Pulled forward and stopped the second time.

This point being past the VFD building at the top, past the driveway that circled and slipped beyond its furthest shadow, past the pine trees at the corner that led to the dirt road, past the doghouse but before his own driveway. He put it in idle and bounced out. Crunching stone back to the yard with the doghouse and burn barrel cut in half. The painted sign declaring Bad Adolph except Bad Adolph had yet to be seen. Steve scanned the perimeter of the house. Kept his ears tuned for pounding feet, his senses honed to the frequency of squeaking canine teeth, aching for blood. Human blood. Why else Bad Adolph?

"Here boy," he almost whispered.

Nothing. So he got down to a knee, nearly put a head to the ground. Nothing in the darkened recess. No stirring, slavering, glowing eyes. Not the fetid stench of wet fur. No litter of bones from previous carnage. No more lair than hollow hole in a tree. And so he stood back up, dusted his jeans.

The storm door to the house creaked open. A head of disheveled hair behind the screen. Steve could only tell it was a woman by the voice.

"You need something?" it said.

Steve cleared his throat. "I don't see your dog."

"Had to put him down."

The door hadn't moved a micron. Steve put his chin to his chest.

"He wasn't doing so good."

And he wouldn't be bad anymore either, but Steve didn't say it. Maybe it balanced out. A dead declaration on a doghouse for a living act of futility. Maybe every raked driveway needed a petless home in proximity. The existence somewhere between and Steve standing on its dirty throat. He shifted his feet as if to ease the pressure. And felt grateful that the pressure in his groin had greatly subsided. Maybe the treatment was working after all and he needed to be at the edge of this pot-holed dirt road to acknowledge it.

He raised his head.

"And an ordered house is a happy house," he said.

"What are you, fucking Confucius?"

And the screen door screamed shut.

So Steve returned to his grumbling truck. And wanted to cry, but he couldn't say why. So he wished it would rain instead. And wash all those stones away.

A few days went by and Steve decided to hit the Station. It was the weekend. He felt better than he had in months. He was almost even getting used to the ole finger up the ass. Well, almost. He had shaved off his mustache and resolved to take his cool pink upper lip out on the town.

188

There was the driveway. As described. Never changing. There were the double doors that slapped like balsam on water. Never changing. There was the usual assortment of sots in stools strung along the edge of the bar. Never changing. There was Steph, pulling on a tap, tits all scrunched up and white as a baby's bottom in winter. Never changing. There was the caterwauling from the billiards room, something in the vein of a drunken begrimed American Supertramp. Never changing. There was the guy with the red face and empty mug butting up against a full one, offering to buy every Puritan who'd fallen off the wagon a beer or shot to commemorate that fall. Never changing. There were the posters of the scantily clad holding wet bottles in climes far too cold for such lack of cover and condensation. Never changing. There was the show on the grainy TV screen in the upper corner blaring how-she-doesn't-love-me-like-she-used-to-and-I'm-sorry-I-fucked-your-sister-at-the-wedding. Never changing. There was the Coors Light in hand. Never changing. The conversations steeped in bravado and bullshit and beet red hilarity. Never changing. There was that goddamn faded out green carpet that was thinner than the arms pulling on the flannel to the even thinner frame of Bones Jones. Never changing. And there was the hollow slap of an empty mug in a puddle on the bar. Never changing. And Steve felt good, at least, for having shaved off that god-awful mustache, because the menthol coolness on his skin meant that he'd at least tried something different. And failed, after all, at even that. Never changing.

So when that angry guy who always scowled at Steve decided once again to fire his scorn anew at him, his ancient enemy, for God-knows-what reason, Steve turned and spit in that scrunched up vinegar face.

"What the fuck, man," the guy said.

Steve leaned in.

"What have you got against me, anyway?"

"Other than you spitting on me?"

But the guy's anger had dissolved to fear. Or a growing fear of sorts.

"Not cool," red-faced man said.

"I'm going to have to ask you to leave, Steve," Steph said. "I'm sorry, but you just can't spit on someone and stay here drinking."

"I'm done with my beer," Steve said, holding the mug aloft like a bloodless holy grail. "And I'm sorry, but it had to be done. This guy," pointing an unbent finger, "is a total douchebag."

"Not cool," red-faced man again. Never changing.

And the crazy guy shook on his stool. Angry and scared and spat upon.

"Man, I'm crazy," he said. "You don't want to mess with me."

"Shove it, you little pissant."

And Steve stared the guy down so that he could only look at his worn shoes propped on his own stool with an empty mug dangling by a finger. Red-faced man even shut his yammering hole. And Steph put her hand on Steve's shoulder.

"Come back another day, Steve," she said. "This guy's not worth it."

"Far out—what a day, a year, a life it is!" from the billiards room.

Steve faced Steph and nodded. He turned and trod along that worn green carpet, pushed through the double doors emblazoned with paperboard promises cut from unfulfilled sweaty dreams. Yet this was no dream. And on the second door slap, Steve breathed deep the fat droplets in the humid air and smiled. Smiled and went to his truck.

Maybe not all things were never changing.

Flushed with triumph and fresh beer, Steve hopped into his truck and punched it downtown. Past the Ford dealership, the green stretch of plots with asphalt tongues licking at the main route's rim, through the odd three way traffic light that no one ever seemed to know how to manage, the beer distributor and tire place, the self service carwash stalls, the plastic-injection plant, the small used car lot, the sub shop across from the market house, the pizza joint that supplied half of Steve's diet, the brickfaced bank flat-headed against the blue sky, the Arby's and Wendy's, the poolhall where only the black went, the Chinese restaurant where everyone went, the four screen cinema that nobody went to anymore, the barber shop that knocked out buzz cuts and the salon that sent out customers in a chemical fog to the uncoifed masses, the church across from the church across from the church across from the church, matched only by the bar across from the bar across from the bar across from the bar where only the whites went. In one of these public house lots, pick one, Steve pulled between white lines and didn't stop until his beefy wheels hit the railroad tie.

Inside now, through unslapping doors, to a sea of shirts with buttons and a surprising lack of denim. Normally Steve avoided this kind of place because he wanted to avoid the inevitable barrage of college jackasses who loud-mouthed in patchy beards and designer jeans. But school was out and the classic rock only pounded that point home. So what was up with all of the professionals? Steve knew the bar down the street, across from the bar beside that napalm salon, would've suited better. That place had craft beer by the bottled billions. This place had light beer cutouts strung along the walls, between beaming flat screens. Flat screen after flat screen. To match the number of bars in this town. To match the number of churches.

And beneath one of these strings, smack dab in the middle of two of those pulsing screens, twisted a stout neck to regard the nattering heads below him. The familiar face of Mr. David King laughing, leaning to listen, agreeing with glass clinks and smiling eyes. He noticed Steve just as he was about to turn and head to any number of other possible watering holes. Watery holes with watery beers. And now Steve's eyes nearly watering with the suddenness. David King's hands waving at him, beckoning him to stride up to the bar, to place himself amidst attentive upturned heads, regarding this regal black chieftain wreathed in paperboard and kissed by angels from the TVs. And wondering why oh why Steve had been regarded worthy of entry.

So he went up to the bar and stuck out his hand. Buttoned-up beings nodded on both sides. A strong grip shaking the meat all the way to the shoulder. An unforced grin. A pale blue shirt. Steve noticed how crisp and fresh this giant was and wiped at a welling eye. Lost in the AC his minor victory from a bar ago. Lost in the presence of a man of greatness who'd have exploits etched in stone if he'd lived in the age of the pharaohs. Steve felt like a shrub rooted to the Nile, a desert away from hieroglyphic glory.

"Steve Shaw," David King said. "What brings you out today?"

"I'm thirsty." And Steve smiled.

David nodded, a head above all others, and grabbed the attention of the bartender.

"What'll it be, Steve?"

And his power was so that he held the attention of the barman, fist rubbing gently into palm, even though there was a score of others down the line waving hands, money and shorter heads. They'd have to wait. As all serfs had to centuries down the line for a monarch in passing.

"Coors Light, I guess."

"Coors Light it is," David said.

The bartender swiped a mug, pulled a handle and passed the beer spilling to the king. And the king handed it to his subject. And Steve bowed his head in thanks.

"So is this the party after the party?" Steve said.

David laughed. "I suppose so." And took a swig.

"So then where you headed?"

And David ordered a refill to his mug. Everyone else at the bar had to wait while the bartender poured another. Even the bodies who'd surrounded their liege and never left kept silent. A special guard, maybe. Silent watchers while their leader deigned to bandy words with a buffoon. But there was no condescension in those unwavering eyes when he'd swung them back to Steve.

"São Paulo," he said.

"Come again?"

"It's in Brazil."

David took another healthy tug.

"So you're not going back to Japan?"

The court arrayed in a fan chuckled. They took sips and shook their heads.

"I think I'll be staying on this side of the hemisphere from now on," David said. "There's a lot opening up in South America, and we just built a new plant." David shrugged. "So they want me to go."

"You certainly made a splash at Green Tree," Steve said. "I mean, when it was the old Green Tree."

"I'd like to think so."

Steve looked into the faces around him. Faces that tolerated and grinned. Awaiting, maybe, the next exhibition. Done with the jester for now. Ready for the dancing women with veils. The feeding of the Christians to lions. The orders to squash the barbarians. A reason to justify standing so close to such fiery greatness. One word and they'd fall on their swords. Right through the line of those neatly pressed shirts.

"Well," Steve said. "Thanks for the beer." He nodded to the others. "I'll let you get back to your friends."

"All right, Steve," David said. "But stay awhile. It's a celebration. You want another you just go up to the bar and tell him it's on me."

Necks nearly cracked turning toward their Lord's decree.

"Really?"

"Absolutely."

"Why?"

And Steve immediately reddened over such rudeness. But he swallowed hard and stood his ground.

"Like I said," David said, waving his mug like a scepter. "It's a celebration."

"Fair enough."

Steve held aloft his own mug, three quarters full, and downed the rest in one gulp. Eyes stinging and watering, mug back out, nodding, turning to the bar to order another. And the great guffaw of David King ripping right across the heads of everyone. He slapped Steve's back. But Steve would have to wait his turn for another. For he was no king. Just a fool. And he felt a fool for even bothering with a refill.

"Hello, Steve."

In the mirror Steve couldn't make out the face to the voice behind him. As if the reflections of the bottles of booze were hiding the interloper. But no interloper, really, for he'd become subsumed by the other itchy palms flexing for fresh supplies. And cut off now, too, from the king and his company. So it was just this disembodied voice that he turned to.

"What're you drinking?"

It was that meek little whelp.

"Oh, hey, Sammy."

Sammy's eyes just got bigger. He pointed.

"So," he said. "What're you drinking?"

"Coors Light."

"Looks good."

And Sammy licked his lips. Steve would swear that on a pallet of bibles. Maybe from one of those churches between bars.

"Yeah, well," Steve said. "They're pouring them."

"Get me one."

Steve cocked his head. Hardened his eyes.

"Like I said, they're—"

"I'd like you to get me one," Sammy said.

And on that same stack of bibles, Steve would bet that Sammy had a knife stashed somewhere. Not that anyone should bet on the Bible.

"Look, Sammy, I know—"

"It's the least you can do, Steve. For all those years you guys picked on me. Always frickin' at me about being a virgin. And retarded."

His nose was running. Steve actually saw it. No bibles necessary.

"Shit, man," Steve said. "We were only joking, didn't mean anything by it."

Sammy wiped his nose with the back of his hand.

"Didn't feel like it," he said. "Get me a beer, Steve."

Steve squared his shoulders. Holding a free beer in his hand. The other almost searching for a way to push out of there. He looked at the wetness on Sammy's hand, under his nose. Saw it glisten like it'd just been shaved. Steve sighed deeply and pulled out a couple of bucks.

"You're right, Sammy." He handed the money over. "We were Grade A assholes."

Sammy winked.

"I don't know, Steve," he said. "You weren't so bad. You were always better than the others."

Steve nodded and let that free hand push him away. Somewhere out into that ever-tightening coil of patrons. He threaded through, skirting David and his retinue, squeezing toward the dart boards on the far wall. To a stool at a corner table. Back against dark paneling. Mirrors. More mirrors. Ever mirrors. People glided around his table and the table next to him and Steve heard a laugh. A laugh he'd heard before. The laugh of a goddess. Confident yet unassuming. Carefree and regal. Queenly. And there was a king in the castle, after all.

A flash of strawberry blond hair. A Celtic queen.

"I know," the voice said. "I actually once did hit myself in the eye with a cabinet door, I'm so clumsy."

"What?"

"Seriously." Flip of the hair. "I was rushing to get dinner started and thinking about the dry cleaning and just blanked out as I opened the door."

"No way."

"My family didn't even question how I got the black eye, they just knew," she said, running on the swelling waves from the AC. "They saw David and said, 'What did she do now?'"

"That's hilarious."

Laughter the sound of angels' feet over harp strings.

Steve drained his beer and stood up. He'd tried not to make a sound but she'd turned to his table and smiled.

"Hello," she said.

And Steve about fell over.

"Hello," he said back.

And felt he should be in a hat with balls hanging off it. A proper, well and thorough fool.

She turned back to her tablemate and continued a conversation that drifted into the ether. Steve walked away, empty mug in hand, ears full of the sound of waves over smooth stones, head empty of all else except the automatic motor skills to head up to the bar, nose full of the scent of something he'd never smell again. The smell of crushed petals, intangible flowers, on the ice-encrusted side of a mountain.

His brain had never worked like this. Near poetry. And so he looked for asses. Tits. Something to help stabilize. And there was plenty of plump flesh to be had. At least for the eyes. But every time he let his gaze slip up or down just the smallest naughty fraction, the scent of a goddess kissing the impossible blue expanse righted his vision. And there he was off again. Flowers. Snow. Mountains. Cloudless skies. Wind. Poetry. Maybe he should've bought his ex-wife flowers, while they were married. Even though they already grew rhododendrons. But then again, she never really deserved flowers. Just maintained them, cut them, put them on her own table. A testament, maybe, to his lack of thought. His lack of love. His lack . . .

His lack of beer.

So he got another Coors Light.

And another.

And the day wore on.

And he didn't feel so outside of everything. Not so unimmersible. Soluble, maybe. Not perfectly, of course. Just enough to take it all in without it changing his chemistry entirely. Not soused. But steeped.

So he had yet another.

Had a few more words with Sammy. Amicable but uncomfortable. But, what the hey. Progress. A few words with some of the newbies. Or relative newbies, since Steve had been at the plant for thirty years. All relative. Progress. A few words with some of the buttoned-up gentry about the game last night and how the Pirates looked to have a promising season, even if they had traded Del Rey. Progress. Even a few words with the bartender, about how people sure must've liked this guy buying all the drinks. And Steve just said that it hadn't been all about the drinks. Progress. And a few words with a woman—yes, a woman—and he didn't think he'd come off as a creep since he hadn't looked down her shirt, or at her ass when she went to the restroom or hadn't asked anything about holding it against him if he'd said she had a nice body. Progress.

Behind him a shadow. The shadow from a mountain. A great bulk that held a queen somewhere on a craggy shoulder. A height distant enough for the thinnest of winds to blow unimpeachable beauty clean through the entire world's skies.

"How you shaping up?" David said, his hand on Steve's shoulder.

"Another beer, I should think," Steve said.

And they both laughed.

At the end of the room, Steve could see David's queen stand up. He knew it was soon time for her to collect him. To continue the adventure on another continent. To maybe conquer it all over again. He knew his time was limited. So he had to get out of himself that minor thing before the creaking of giant vessels unmoored and sailed to lands of glaciers and penguins. At least Steve thought South America had penguins. But before he could forget, he forced himself to remember. Out loud.

"Hey, you know that thing I said?" Steve said.

David didn't move his hand. Just squeezed lightly.

"Don't worry about it," he said.

"I just . . ."

The queen seemed to be wrapping up her conversation. Feet pointed toward her husband. Hair not blowing out like the girls in the TVs plastered all round the bar. Yet, she had no need for fans. For make believe. She had an honest-to-goodness mountain to stand upon. He'd catch all the wind she could possibly need. And now that mountain was implacable. Inscrutable. Patient.

"You know, for some reason I've harbored this grudge against you," Steve said. "And I can't remember why."

David removed his hand, took a sip. Waited for Steve to go on. And so Steve went on.

"I wasted so much time."

A grin split that great rocky being, from one curve of the planet to the other.

"Why'd you think I bought you the beer?" he said.

"I just wanted you to know," Steve said.

He put the mug on the bar. He stood up and quickly walked away. He didn't look back. Didn't waver in his decision to let it all rest. Didn't need to see the strawberry tresses crash against the sides of an unmovable force. Didn't need to watch as they stood, too, and walked out that bar forever. Hand in hand. Man and wife. Off to shake the crust on a continent that Steve wasn't completely sure had penguins on it or not. But no matter. He could imagine it all. And that was enough. And that imagination was like the smell all caught up in the cavities of his head. Caught up and kept there until his last exhale, he knew.

Something wholly new, that.

And that was progress enough.

Supper time, a late supper for Steve, came a knocking at the door. So Steve answered it, wiping wet hands on his jeans. In the porch light glare he watched his son shuffle his feet.

"What, you got to pee?"

"Actually," Kevin said. "I do."

Steve stepped aside for his son. The table laid with a dirty plate and bowl. Crinkled paper napkin. Big blue Tupperware container half full of salad. A glass of red wine.

"Am I interrupting something?"

"Just finishing up dinner," Steve said. "You want some?"

"You made dinner?"

And he looked his dad square in the eyes.

Steve shrugged and said, "There's salad." He pointed toward the kitchen. "And spaghetti. It's sauce from a jar, but pretty good, actually."

"And you shaved your stache."

Fingers automatically went to cover the naked skin over the lip. "Yeah." Then dropped just as quickly. "So?"

Kevin smiled. "Well, you look less like a cocksucker and more like yourself."

"Not that," Steve said. "You want food?"

"No, no." Still smiling. "I'm good."

"Thought you said you had to piss," Steve said.

"Yes, right."

And Kevin headed up the stairs toward the bathroom. Steve went to the stairwell but his son had disappeared. He yelled up.

"Takes one to know one."

"Yeah, yeah."

Then the closing of a door. Steve stared into silence a moment. He turned and went to gather the dishes. Brought them to the sink and started rinsing. Everything stacked to the side so he could wash it later. The salad closed up and stowed inside the fridge. A swipe at his glass of wine and plopping on the kitchen counter. A running of water over dish soap and the ensuing froth. He deposited the dishes in water so hot he had to withdraw from being scalded. The bubbles covering the entire surface of the water. Out of sight, for the moment, so he wiped his hands on the towel draped over the stove handle. Grabbed up his wine and took a sip.

The creak of the stairs from his son's descent.

"So how'd everything come out?" Steve said.

Kevin rolled his eyes. Actually rolled them. Melodrama rubbed off from his mother.

"And now you're drinking wine?"

Steve looked at it in the light. The color of blood before it seeps into blackest night. And he almost groaned at the encroachment of that poetry again. Those goddamned poetic flourishes that wouldn't settle to the ground.

"The doctor says a glass of red wine a day is good for the heart."

"He say this when his finger was up your ass?"

Steve almost bit the glass. "What?"

And Kevin couldn't help notice the more than unusual pause.

"Don't they all do that?" he said. "When you old farts get to your age."

Steve gulped hard and placed the glass on the counter. He turned to the sink and started washing the dishes.

"So what brings you out tonight?" he said.

"I was just at Mom's."

Kevin watching the methodical working hands. Rub rinse stack. Back into the water.

"So how is that ancient vampire?"

"You'll be happy to know that she walks with a cane."

Rub rinse stack.

"Why would that make me happy?"

"Because she doesn't need it."

"Of course."

Nodding. Rub rinse stack.

"Just told her some news."

"You mean to tell me she didn't know you fancied boys?"

"Pop . . ."

Rub rinse stack.

"Dad."

So Steve stopped. Turned to his son. Let the rub rinse stack cycle out into the water. Like a press at the end of its shift.

"I'm moving."

"What?"

"To Austin."

Steve gulped hard again, but he hadn't swallowed any liquid. So he wiped his hands on his jeans and grabbed the glass of wine. Anchor enough.

"My roommate," Kevin said, "my old roommate says there are lots of jobs out there. That it's booming."

"Just like São Paulo."

"Huh?"

Steve took a sip and looked at the distorted face of his son through the glass.

"I bet they got a lot of wine in Brazil," Steve said.

"To go with all that sun and sand and naked flesh."

"You did hear that I was going to move to Texas?"

Steve's lips in a straight line. He closed his eyes a second. Then drained half the glass of blood in one pull. He put the empty under the suds. And pushed it to the bottom and felt the sear burn up his knuckles.

"All that way, my boy?" he said.

"Well." Kevin's eyes dropped. "There's nothing going on here. Nothing for me."

Steve nodded his head. "It's true. It's all dying. Nothing new."

"I didn't mean that, Pop."

"I know."

Steve's eyes looked as if about to crack. Like too much air had blown straight in and left them cold and brittle. The hammer of the news ready to break them to rubble.

"This is an opportunity for me," Kevin said.

"Of course it is," Steve said. "You should take it. This town's turning more ghost-like by the day."

"You all right, Pop?"

Before fissuring, before waters could burst those old bloodshot dams asunder, Steve reached out a hand and put it on his son's shoulder. He gripped, feebly, for he needed the strength to utter the words. And to look straight and true and not waver.

"You know I'm OK with everything?" he said. "That I love you the way you are."

And now Kevin swallowed hard.

"How much of that wine have you had?"

But tears had already fallen down Kevin's cheeks. And since there wasn't any point in pretense anymore, and since Steve couldn't tell the next time he'd see his son, he pulled him toward him and squeezed harder than he'd ever squeezed anything in his life.

And cried like a baby. A stinking little baby.

Another day, another time, in the same town, the

same old town, Steve forded the flat nose of his truck through the sewage treatment plant's greatest reek of the summer. Barely passing the curve of the bridge he slowed at the spectacle of blinking blues at the intersection. Slowed then stopped. Beyond sight of the sewage plant. Fully immersed in the city's fetid vapors. Police by their cars and directing traffic. Orange cones and auxiliary cops in neon vests. Two lanes completely closed down. The other two used to allow the populace to be squeezed out in peristalsis. Horns honking and heat waving off the tarmac. Windows rolled down and radios blaring. A short man, unshaved and grimy, a miniature version of Bones Jones, flapped his arms and pumped his little legs. All the authority a man could muster in an auxiliary vest. Pointing to people and cars and pathways, uncaring if anyone was paying attention. As if the weight of responsibility lay squarely on that squat frame and needed no validation, no gesture or signal, no crack in the sky or bolt thrown from the heavens. And on one of these all important rounds, Steve yelled out the window from on high.

"What's the hold up?"

Restless legs glued to pavement. Head swiveling as if he'd had no neck. And maybe there wasn't. Just caked motor oil and scruff. Eyes lit on Steve. Head raised and nose shadowed by the brim of his FRAM cap. Feet unstuck and plodded to the flank of Steve's steaming beast.

"The bowling alley caught on fire," the man said.

A high-pitched voice. Totally undermining his ephemeral leadership. Like the source of flame that was found not to be a source at all. Phlogiston. Fizzled out somewhere in the fatter molecules of heat, sweat and funk. The man was only doing his job, after all, so Steve just let it rest.

"How?"

The man looked down at the mass bulged round the flashing lights. He turned back to Steve, head back and

203

still gazing along the line of the soiled brim.

"Guess you'll have to read the morning paper," he said.

"No known source."

The little man shrugged. "Just be ready to move along when it's your turn." And he whipped around and marched down the line of cars.

Another car came tearing up the lane to the left. It came to a screeching halt just opposite Steve's door. The lane was meant for traffic coming the other way, just now given the flip of the sign and the OK by a bevy of auxiliary police flapping wings in circles. And arms were flapping out the car windows beside the chugging muscle of Steve's truck. Slender, tan, hairless arms. Belting away on some melody blaring from the car. And laughter. One girl shook out her wavy blond locks, hands to the door frame, and Steve could see right down her shirt. No bra. Massive tits. She yelled something and he watched those mountains shudder under fabric. A hand from behind brought her back and then up. Her face went crooked and she flipped him off, but Steve kept staring anyway.

DIRTY OLD MAN, but he didn't care.

And slapping steps on the pavement finally wrenched his vision from the smooth, bursting paps fit to challenge the Himalayas. And those feet attached to a pointing finger. And that finger just below a bellowing mouth. And that mouth just shy a shadow of the brim that sat shorter than Steve's elbow on his door.

More laughter. Tits forever gone. But the image of snow-capped mountains would run over and over in his head. But for now the laughter was whisked away in hurried reverse, the whirring and slap slapping, and the car nearly backed into another as it spun, headed in the opposite direction, and sped away. The little chugging legs came to a stop and he put hands to knees and panted. Before he stood up, Steve swore the man put those filthy fingers to his nose and sniffed.

Maybe this guy had started the fire. An oil fire. Grease fire. But then Steve knew that that was too big a task for such a little man. Grand schemes, like grand crimes, first-degree arsons, were perpetrated by men of great dreams, if not great vision. Lust overstepping the sublime every time. And a man content with sniffing oil from his fingers would never dig into the heart of real conflagration. Satisfied with the charred, the sooty remainders. Not the spark of the flame. Not the origin. The aftermath. The carbon.

The wail of a fire engine ripped the air to tatters. The auxiliary cop stopped inhaling long enough to run on ahead. The sign flipped and his lane started moving. And so Steve released the brake and eased the gas, up the hill, slipping past the blinking blues, beyond the fog barrier of the town's offal, out to the edge where the last car in line sat mute and ignorant, the face beneath the windshield crinkled in consternation.

Sucker.

And Steve was a sucker, too. Stuck in a town in a job in a moment where no one ever considered imaginary chemicals to very real fires. But at least he had the wind in his face.

Outside the apartment complex where his son had lived, Steve parked in front of the big green dumpster. A bureau had been left behind for lack of space and lack of need. But it was still in good shape, so Steve said he'd come pick it up and store it in the basement. He put down the gate. Removed all of the drawers and stacked them in the bed. Empty, the bureau wasn't impossibly heavy so he worked it up to the edge and hauled it in. Careful not to drag it. Everything snug by the cab and secured with bungee cords. He hopped out and slammed home the gate.

And then heard a peculiar sound. Not peculiar, exactly. More strange for being out of context. A cat mewing in a tin can. He looked under the truck. Nothing. He approached the dumpster and the pathetic whine got louder. The metal door grinding as it was thrust aside. In the darkened interior, among the rotting remains of the apartment tenants, sat a cardboard box. And in that box stood a kitten looking up. Shaky legs and bulging eyes. It mewed again, stepped forward and stopped before the box could topple and slide down the refuse pile. Nearly lost at the bottom with castoffs, broken objects, shifting human scree. It hunched down and peeped at Steve.

"Who the hell would throw away a cat?"

Before the anger could take Steve full in the mind and limbs, before the blood could pump piping hot through the veins, he reached in and grabbed the kitten from the box. He backed away from the dumpster and held the reaching animal to the light. Gray with black stripes and white paws. Mewing appeals. Whiskers straight out. Its claws digging lightly into the flesh. He brought the kitten to his chest and cradled it. He reached back into the dumpster and retrieved the empty box. Made his way to the truck, opened the passenger door and plopped the box on the seat. He rounded the grill and opened the driver door. He jumped in and gently deposited the kitten inside the box.

"Don't worry," Steve said. "It's just for the ride."

Little white paws gripped the cardboard flaps. Eyes big and wet like puddles after a downpour. Any vestige of Steve's anger dissolving into those glinting pools.

A universal solvent. Compassion and need meeting on the bench seat of a truck.

"Let's go home," Steve said to the kitten.

He turned the key and felt the motor roar like the heart of a great protecting cat.

ACKNOWLEDGMENTS

Twelve years in the making. Well, actually started twelve years ago and then summarily stowed away. For lack of information or lack of drive to finish it. In any case, when I revisited *Phlogistics* earlier this year, I was surprised how much I liked it and how little I had to change. I guess that's what comes with writing it simply and being faithful to my experiences in shop jobs and the cast of characters I'd met there. A time capsule and a greater resolution now than then – more backbone, less spirit maybe. So I guess I've got my younger, weaker self to thank – for the painstaking notes, for the vision, for keeping the heart of the story alive with hydraulic fluid and twelve-year-old slurry. Just as I'm thankful to all those co-workers in the fog of memory.

To those who continue to help me: Jamie Szymanski for yet another editing endeavor. Anna Mann for taking the pictures. To Stanley Newton for being a far more patient model than me. To Missy for making the cover simple and yet not underwhelming. I am overwhelmed by everyone's graciousness, honesty and dedication to your craft. And yes, Stanley, blank-faced sitting is a skill.

At the end I'm just happy that there was something to the spark after all. Phlogiston is a very real thing, even if disproved by science.

Made in the USA
Charleston, SC
01 October 2015